THE BLUE STAR
cookbook

THE BLUE STAR

cookbook:
Try This At Home

James W. Davis, Jr.

with Molly Wingate

THE BLUE STAR

cookbook: *Try This At Home*

Printed in Canada

ISBN: 1-887128-01-8

Cover, book design, and photography by Don Goede unless otherwise noted.
Indexing by Southwinds Indexing Service.
Interior Blue Star photographs by Mike Jackson.

For copies of this cookbook contact:

THE BLUE STAR

1645 South Tejon St.
Colorado Springs
CO 80906
(719) 632-1086

www.thebluestar.net
(multiple copy discounts available)

Table of Contents

Foreword..vii
Acknowledgements...viii-x
Introduction..xi
How to Use This Book..xiii
Words from our Kitchen Testers..xv
The Contributors..xvii
History of the Blue Star..xix

Tapas
Smoked Salmon Brie en Croûte..2
Stuffed Prince Edward Island Mussels..3
Thai Shrimp Cakes and Table Sauce...4-5
Coconut Peanut Shrimp Satay..6
Cheese Stuffed Poblano Pepper Wraps (vegetarian)..............................7
Athena's Goat Cheese Terrine (vegetarian)...8
Cuban Beef on Sugar Cane Skewers..9
Mojo Marinated Chicken Quesadillas..10

Salads
Tahini Vinaigrette over Spinach with Grilled Vidalia Onions and Toasted Pine Nuts (vegan)..................................12
Red Leaf Lettuce and Asparagus Bundles with Raspberry Vinaigrette (vegan)..................................13
Institutional Salad (vegetarian)...14
Company Salad (vegetarian)...15
Mixed Greens with Dried Fruit Cambozola Roulade, Rhubarb Compote, and Currant Port Vinaigrette (vegetarian)..................16-17
Bocconcini Caprese Salad (vegetarian)..18
Smoked Salmon and Black Pepper Strawberries on Spinach................19
Warm Cabbage with Prosciutto Vinaigrette..20
Herbed Crostini (vegetarian)...21
The Vinaigrettes..22

Soups, Stocks, Sauces, and Toppings
Swiss Onion Soup..26
Butternut Bisque (vegetarian)..27
Chicken Lime Tortilla Soup...28-29
Carrot Cumin Soup (vegetarian)...30
Jamaica Jerk Conch Chowder..31
Shrimp Essence...32
Chicken Stock...33
Vegetable Stock (vegan)...34
Veal Stock, Demi-glace, Glace de Viande..35-36
Mushroom Stock (vegan)..37
Sun Dried Tomato Pesto (vegetarian)...37
Chipotle Aioli (vegetarian)...38
Bomb Sauce (vegan)..38
James Davis's Hollandaise (vegetarian)...39
Persillade (vegan)...40
Warlock Onions (vegan)..40

Entrées

Almond Rosemary Crusted Salmon..42
Parmesan Halibut with Red Grapes...43
Tito Puente Tilapia Tacos...44
Poached Ahi Sashimi with Cucumber Salad..45-46
Jimmy's Shrimp Creole..47-48
Louisiana Crab Cakes..49
Crab Stuffed Portobello Mushrooms..50
Grilled Quail with Tuscan White Beans...51-52
Thai Duck with Sugar Snap Peas..53
Grilled Lamb with Pine Nut Compound Butter...54-55
Laughing Lab Beef Chili...56
Stuffed Beef Tenderloin Filet...57
Steak au Poivre...58
Gorgonzola Beef Tips..59
Wild Mushroom Loops with Asparagus and Red Burgundy Gastrique (vegetarian)....................60-61
Just Warm Greek Pasta (vegetarian)...62
Moussaka Deconstructa (vegetarian)..63-64

Sides

House Mashers (vegetarian)..76
The Rice Page (vegan)..77
Corn Confetti (vegan)..78
Fruity Guacamole (vegan)..78
Regina's Black Beans (vegan)...79
Pico de Gallo (vegan)..80

Desserts

(all vegetarian)

Chocolate Bread Pudding with Tuaca Caramel...82
Banana Death..83
Chocolate Espresso Lava Cake with Raspberry Syrup..84-85
Corleone...86
Chocolate Cheesecake..87
Buttermilk Brûlée...88
Tuaca Caramel..89
French Crème..89
Gingerbread Cake with Raspberry Salsa and Whipped Ginger Cream..90-91

Gathering Ingredients...93-94
Glossary of Cooking Terms...95-96
List of Sponsors...97-98
Beer and Wine Index...99-100
Index...101-107

Foreword

The first day I met Joe Coleman, he told me that he was going to own a very successful restaurant in a few years, and he wanted to learn all he could from me. Usually, I chuckle to myself when people say that they want to own a successful restaurant; I know how difficult it really is to do it. But I didn't laugh at Joe.

Two years after tossing pizzas for 12 hours a day for me at Poor Richard's Restaurant, Joe talked at least ten friends into loaning him at least $1,000 each, promising them their money back with good interest in a year. With no real business experience, little cooking expertise, and a sketchy knowledge of wines, Joe opened the first Blue Star restaurant in a beautiful old brick building, across the street from Surplus City in the Old Colorado City neighborhood of Colorado Springs. He paid his creditors back in eighteen months, and the Blue Star was a smashing success. In two years, he outgrew his Old Colorado City location, borrowed a lot more money from a bank than he originally cajoled from friends, and moved the Blue Star into the cavernous Ross Auction building on South Tejon Street. The rest is history.

The Blue Star Restaurant ranks as one of the finest, most original dining experiences in the state of Colorado. The atmosphere is hip, urbane, warm, and elegant. The Blue Star's chefs constantly one-up themselves for creativity, presentation, and taste. Blue Star's white-shirted, black-tied servers are some of the best in the business — friendly, helpful, unobtrusive, and efficient. Blue Star's wine cellar is legendary in the region. The place is packed with "special occasion" diners and regulars who have been patronizing the Blue Star for years. And in the midst of all the wonderful smells, tastes, atmosphere, and service hovers Joe Coleman, "pizza-tosser extraordinaire," walking up to tables, grabbing regulars on their shoulders with his loving, iron grip, making sure that every detail of the Blue Star is working as it should.

Richard Skorman

Richard Skorman
Owner Poor Richard's Restaurant
Colorado Springs Councilman

Richard Skorman

www.bluefoxphotography.com

Acknowledgements

James W. Davis, Jr.

First I want to thank the Davis and Hester families in South Georgia for all their southern charm and root knowledge of food. Thanks, too, to Dan Bailey for the Cuban influences and to Ms. Guzman, my babysitter, for the Peruvian liver, pan-seared rare, at the end of a hard day playing when I was nine.

Thanks to Joseph Coleman for persevering with me through it all; may I live to see his hair all gray. Thanks to Tyler Schiedel for helping me believe in my skills and talents. Thanks to Andy Marsh for the Bomb Sauce. And thanks to Matt Daniluk for complaining so I didn't have to and for keeping the sorbet containers clean.

I want to thank Molly Wingate for pushing me in my mother's absence and Cari Davis for being with Joe. Thanks to Matt Shea for the horse hook grab and to Matt Reid for proving that you can change if you choose to. And thanks to Jason "Leron" Davis for all the brotherly love, and to Courtney "Reverend Horton Heat" my little sister, and Misty "Conquistador" Davis, my other little sister, for cooking with me a lot. Thanks to the Abare clan, and a big thanks to my stepfather, Chris James, for putting me through school.

Molly Wingate

I want to thank all the kitchen testers who volunteered to prepare and to eat the recipes in this book. Their creative and critical feedback helped me know when to keep, cut, or revise a recipe.

Richard Agee, Colorado Springs
Tony Bevis, Colorado Springs
Mary Ellen Davis, Colorado Springs
Jean Echevarria, Colorado Springs
Corinne Murphy, White Plains, New York
Terry Schwartz, Colorado Springs
Holly Sims, San Miguel Allende, Mexico
Floyd Sklaver, Portland, Oregon
Cindy Utt, Manitou Springs

Mary Ellen Davis responded to the words as well as the food in the book. Her willingness to read anything I sent her provided a much-appreciated touchstone, and her ideas were always right on point. Don Goede, book designer, illustrator, and photographer, helped turn my ideas about the book into the object you have in your hands. Brian, Gavin, and Aidan Murphy were good sports for eating all the recipes I tried out at home. I am grateful for their unflagging support as this project took shape and, occasionally, took over my life. Thanks, too, to Scott Lincoln and Brenda Mientka for letting us take pictures in their homes.

Finally, I want to thank Joseph E. Coleman, Jr. and James W. Davis, Jr. for trusting me to be the midwife for their dream of creating a Blue Star cookbook.

Joe Coleman

So many people deserve our thanks for helping to build and sustain The Blue Star. It's hard to express my gratitude in a few short paragraphs. That said….here goes. Thank you to….

Richard, Merrie Lynne, Christopher, and *Michael Detoy:* for your early support, long before The Blue Star opened. *Richard*…for reading and providing feedback on the business plans. *Christopher*…for designing the logo.

Peggy and David Taylor, Mary and Tim Cobb: for constant support throughout the years, your continuous patronage, and great ideas. For all the people you introduced to The Blue Star.

Barry and Cathy Nolan: for your week in, week out vegetarian inspiration.

David and Kaye Caster of Old Town Guest House: for your patronage, and for sending so many guests our way.

Susan and Michael Grace and *Tim and Susan Patterson*: for your high standards, frank feedback, and consistent support.

Steve and Janice Meylan and *Tim and Kelly Kisielnicki*: for your patience during Kelly's birthday party (when I cooked), for having the craziest parties with Crazy Chuck, and for your loyal support.

The Tessarowicz Family: TGIT...Thank God It's Thursday or Thank God It's the Tessarowicz's....for joining us each and every Thursday.

Dr. Bryan and Amy Carr: for coming in on Sunday nights, for Booker's Manhattans, and for inspiring James Davis.

To some of our favorite doctors who threw large parties, and some who introduced us to pharmaceutical representatives:

Dr. James and Betty Ann Albert
Dr. Warren and Bobbie Goldstein
Dr. Patrick and Chris Faricy (and his whole group)
Dr. Robin Johnson and Dr. Tim Rummel
Dr. Ken and Kathleen Gamblin

A special thanks to *Dr. Patrick and Chris Faricy*: for inspiring us to find our current location.

To all of our favorite lawyers and spouses, great Christmas parties...if you ever need anything solved, one of these will get it done. If you need the Dennis...God help you!!

Dennis and Debbie Hartley
David and Gaynelle Mize

Scott and Ann Blackmun
John Cook
Linda Cook
Barkley and Diane Heuser
Brian Murphy and Molly Wingate
Ray and Patty Deeny

Tad Davis: "The Man" for your help, day one, orchestrating the demolition of the first space, ensuring the safety of our dedicated volunteers, and for being a constant resource for both advice and tools.

Ralph and Chandler Bruning: Ralph...for his custom metal work. Chandler... for his inspired cooking and team work.

Lisa Hazelton and Stuart Miller: for letting me practically live with you as the first Blue Star was being built, and for being loving and supportive friends who have become my family.

Dan Foster and the Mountain Chalet crew: for great support and great parties.

Jeff Frees of Coaltrain Liquors and Alan Manley: "Wine Gods," we did not know what we didn't know!!! Thank you for coming in on Sunday and Monday nights and for educating us about wine. We are still learning.

Jim and Earl Turnipseed of La Baguette: Jim....for your business advice, and Earl....for carrying me in the early days.

Doug Logue and Kathy McQuillen: for your design and custom wood work.

Gil Johnson and Dusty Loo: two great friends and wise elders for your advice, time, knowledge on everything from construction cost to fine wine.

Rich Schell and Greg Wragge: for beautiful flowers, continued support, great feedback, and your color palette.

I'd like to thank some of my previous employers, each of whom taught me much and allowed me to learn on their clock:

Ron Kramer
Bobby Kramer & Bob Butler
The Broadmoor
Dan Cross & Linda LaFollette
Richard Skorman
Kimball Bayles

I want to thank all the employees for their vision of what food and service could and should be. There is not enough space for all their names!!! Thank You!

There are some others who not only worked, but gave it all they had when everything was on the line. It was us against the world for a long time. *Matt Shea, Matt Reed, Dan Bailey, David Rice, James D., Matt D., Ben, Will, Mark, Ricky, Pat, Drew, Michelle, Robin, Heather, Dawn, and Michael.* I believed that it was possible; they where the ones who made it so. May everyone on a mission be blessed with working with people of this caliber.

And for the current management team and staff, special thanks for being able to manage it better than ever: *Billy Adams, Tyler Schiedel, and Emily Vollmer* and 40 other hardworking, dedicated souls.

In 1995 there were a handful of people who took a risk and loaned me between $1,000 and $5,000. Each person helped the Blue Star become a reality, to help me achieve my dream:

Greg & Gypsy Ames   *Mary Coleman*
Cari Davis   *Matthew Daniluk*
Brad Gibson   *Rachel Hess*
Alan Manley   *Bruce McGrew*
Dr. Ed & Kerri Schmitt   *Chris White*
Dan Jenkins & Lauren Bynum
Ian and Mary Merkle Scotland

In 1998, three people provided exceptional support for our expansion:
Beth Murdaugh, M.D., Jack and Lisa O'Donnell

For my parents... Thank you for teaching me:
  • the value of a strong work ethic,
  • a firm handshake,
  • the value of money,
  • the difference between what we want and what we need.

Uncle Chuck from National: thank you for telling your boss you had a check from us…when we knew you didn't.

The Colorado College: For my dear alma mater (just kidding), I thank you for your continued support. Please keep interviewing! Some of our best have been some of your best.

Anyone in the restaurant business knows how painful and expensive equipment breakage/malfunctions can be. From day one, we've been blessed with *Refrigeration Dave and Larry San George*—two of the most skilled, the greatest, I can't say enough, professionals in the business.

Introduction

The Blue Star Cookbook: Try This at Home provides experienced and novice cooks with great recipes and helpful information to create smashingly successful lunch and dinner parties for their families and friends. We've gathered together recipes from the past 10 years of cooking at The Blue Star and picked out the best ones for mildly ambitious home cooks. Then we asked people with average kitchens to prepare the dishes. Their successes told us when we had a winner.

The criteria for a recipe to make it in the book were:

> The ingredients are available in the Pikes Peak
> > Region.
> It took no more time than an inspired cook would
> > spend on a special meal.
> Equipment usually found in a well-stocked home
> > kitchen was adequate.
> Typical residential stoves, ovens, and grills created
> > great results.
> Our recipe testers were thrilled with the results.

These recipes will be pretty darn good the first time you cook them, and they will get even better as you learn them, change them, and adopt them as yours. Some recipes rely on other recipes in the book, some stand alone. Some are good for your health, and some you shouldn't tell your doctor about. All are elegant, inventive, and delicious.

These dishes are not intended for everyday fare. They are for special events, (not that Thursday can't be a special event). We didn't aim for quick and easy – although some are easy and a few of them of quick. We want to show you how to make very good, creative meals from scratch. To that end, you will find recipes for soup stocks and for sauces which serve as the bases for other dishes. You can buy the stock or sauce if you wish, but if you want to learn how to make your own, the recipe is here. The food you serve your family and friends will reflect the time and love you put in.

Just in case the idea of making recipes such as chocolate ganache from scratch makes you a tad nervous, we built a little support into every recipe. You will find chef's notes from James Davis. You will find a list of any out-of-the-ordinary kitchen equipment you will need; we tell you how long it will take you to prepare the dish and if you need to prepare anything in advance; and we provide suggestions for what wines or beers you might like to serve. There is a glossary of cooking terms in the back, along with a list of specialty ingredients, what they are, and what kind of stores we found them in.

We think that you will have fun cooking with this book and that your family and guests will be thrilled. We hope *The Blue Star Cookbook: Try This at Home* acts as a springboard for your own culinary creations.

Bon appétit,

James W. Davis, Jr. and Molly Wingate

James and Molly in the Colorado sun.

How to use this book

Read the recipes through at least once so you don't discover any last-minute surprises. As with any directions, you can use the recipes as strict guides or as general guidelines, whichever you prefer. We've included how difficult the recipe is, how much time to allow, and any out-of-the-ordinary equipment you might need. We have also included serving suggestions and wine/beer pairings. In the back, we have listed what kinds of stores carry the specialty ingredients.

If you need more information, please feel free to contact us through The Blue Star, 1645 S. Tejon St., Colorado Springs, Colorado 80906; 719-632-1086, or write to James and Molly via email at: cookbook@thebluestar.net.

Difficulty ratings:
With each recipe, you will find a difficulty rating represented by one, two, or three blue stars; one is the easiest, three is the most difficult. These ratings consider the amount of time, the number of steps, the number of ingredients to be gathered, and the amount of patience required to create the dish.

Preparation Times:
The preparation times reflect the time the recipe takes once you have gathered the ingredients. We assumed that, like our kitchen testers, you will get in the kitchen and get busy. For a few of the more complicated dishes, we have suggested an order of preparation to make the best use of your time.

Special Equipment:
If you need something a little out of the ordinary, we listed it. For example, not everyone keeps parchment paper in stock, so if you need it to make the recipe, we alert you to it near the top of the page.

Wine pairings:
In selecting wines, we made an effort to list two options for each dish. The first option will be something readily available at better wine shops at a price of less than $15. The second wine will be a bit more expensive, and may require some hunting, or possibly a special order from your regular wine shop. These wines will generally be over $20, but worth the additional expense due to their added complexity, intensity, and uniqueness.

We have also made recommendations of wines from around the world for two reasons. First, the recipes are collected from around the world, and they often match best with wines local to them. Second, just like the cookbook, the pairings provide opportunities to try something new.

With that in mind, please remember every person's sense of taste is different. Personal preferences may outweigh anything recommended here. If you like cabernet with your halibut, go for it. But for those finding their way (including the wine guy for this cookbook, Drew Robinson, who has been doing this for almost 20 years) these recommendations may be helpful.

Beer Pairings:
You may be surprised to find beer pairings in this book. The many styles of well-crafted beer available in this country offer an incredible array of flavors — caramelized sweetness, roast, fruit, floral bitterness, coffee, nuts…the list goes on. We think beer is a more appropriate accompaniment to some of the dishes. Try these pairings and you will be exposed to a whole new world of flavor.

Because this may be a new concept to you, we have included a style description with our beer recommendations. Where possible, we encourage you to experiment with a local version of the style if available because, as with ingredients, freshest is always best. As with the wine suggestions, use these recommendations as a start, not a finish. And above all, have fun with it.

A few miscellaneous pointers:

About knives. The number one chef's tool, aside from hands, is a good, razor-sharp knife — the kind that can nick your finger if you aren't careful. Everything about preparing an elegant meal goes better with a good knife. From creating a perfectly diced, ripe tomato for a salad to removing a cheesecake from a spring form pan, you'll be happier with your results when you use a good, sharp knife. So while you're trying to decide which recipe to try first, go sharpen your knives. Call it purposeful procrastination.

Salt and pepper to taste. At the Blue Star, we like to be heavy on pepper. What do you like? That is the taste to aim for. When we say, "to taste," we are letting you know that you might not need much of either, so go slowly, adding just a little bit of salt and pepper at a time.

Despite the concerns about too much salt in our diets, salt remains one of the basic seasonings in a kitchen. When used in moderation, it brightens and flavors food in a healthful way. There are lots of kinds of salt out there: sea salt, kosher salt, iodized salt and so on. We suggest that you use whichever salt you like, but leave the door open to try different kinds. Kosher salt is easy to distribute evenly with your fingers; iodized feels nice in your fingers when sprinkling; sea salt can be intensely salty so a little can go far.

There are at least as many kinds of peppercorns as there are salts. In this book, "pepper" refers to ground black pepper. If you prefer a mixture of red, white and black peppercorns, that's fine.

Fresh vs. dried herbs:
Whenever you can, use fresh herbs. The flavor and fragrance will add depth to your cooking. Occasionally we refer to dried herbs because it would be a waste to buy fresh ones to boil in a soup. Always try to add fresh herbs toward the end.

James W. Davis,

Blue Star Catering;
Hope you've got insurance.

Words from our kitchen testers and tasters

These are really good recipes that gave me room to add my own preferences. I enjoyed making them.
—Richard Agee

Some of these recipes have become things I make all the time. The *Just Warm Greek Pasta*, for instance, is very versatile.
—Jean Echevarria

I have never cooked anything with demi-glace, much less made it from beef broth. I loved learning how to do it, and the *Gorgonzola Beef Tips* were terrific. Also the *Company Salad* is to die for, yummm.
—Cindy Utt

Dessert is not my area; I don't even really like dessert. But kitchen testing the *Buttermilk Brûlée* recipe has given me confidence. It took time, but it worked wonderfully.
—Molly Wingate

I had never used tahini before, but I really liked the results when I made the *Tahini Viniagrette* salad dressing.
—Corinne Murphy

I made the *Almond Rosemary Crusted Salmon,* and it is just as good as at the restaurant. For cooks like me that have sweet and hot paprika, it would be a good idea to say what kind to use in the recipe. I also made the recipe for *Thai Duck with Sugar Snap Peas:* fabulous!!!!
—Terry Schwartz

I loved the *Cheese Stuffed Poblano Pepper Wraps*. I also loved the *Warm Cabbage with Proscuitto Viniagrette* – I used serrano ham instead of prosciutto because prosciutto is hard to find in my little Mexican town.
—Holly Sims

The *Chocolate Cheesecake* was a huge success; there wasn't a crumb left over by the end of the night. Also the *Crab Stuffed Portobello Mushroom* recipe is simple, filling, and quite delicious. Now I want to make the crab cakes, so send me the *Chipotle Aioli* and *Saffron Rice* recipes.
—Floyd Sklaver

The *Steak au Poivre* was a great hit – I served it with baked potatoes. And the *Carrot Cumin Soup* was quite colorful and good.
—Richard Agee

"Anymore of those lava cakes?"
—Aidan Murphy, taster

"Mom, what can we have for dinner that goes with Blue Star *House Mashers*?"
—Gavin Murphy, taster

Joe Coleman

The Contributors

The Chef

James W. Davis, Jr.'s grandfather first inspired him to explore food. Posey Dangerfield Hester had all sorts of Chinese noodles, liver pâtés, and clam dips in his kitchen. He had soup stocks, little jars of sauces, and Japanese foods in his refrigerator. As a five-year-old, James started plundering the cupboards. Rumor has is that he would do anything for a Japanese curry and green onion omelet prepared by Grandpa, especially if James got to watch the preparation.

By elementary school, James was doctoring up canned soup with garlic and peppers. He also learned the hard way not to try to hard boil eggs in the microwave; an egg in its shell explodes! In second grade, James sometimes helped out in the kitchen of the restaurant his stepfather managed. He washed dishes, but he also cracked flat after flat of eggs to prepare enough scrambled eggs to fill three 5-gallon buckets. Eventually he was allowed to work with a knife, preparing romaine for salads. After he was done, he often slipped into the refrigerator and to help himself to the Neapolitan cream pies.

James comes from a family of good cooks. Nana Davis had big slices of fresh tomatoes and Vidalia onions in the summer. Uncle Julian always cooked up doves in a stew with grits. And James' father, a good Southern cook, had a way with squirrels in a pressure cooker. Mama Molly moved into healthier foods as James hit high school and taught him about whole grains and lots of vegetables. He claims his childhood left him addicted to sweet Kool Aid and Southern sweet tea so ropey that it stands on its own.

In 1992, James graduated with an associate's degree in culinary arts from Johnson and Wales University in Charleston, South Carolina. Everywhere he went, he learned what there was to know about the food being prepared: pizza, gumbo, crab. He learned about seafood from Certified Executive Chef Tim Creehan in Destin, Florida. After moving to Colorado Springs, he got a call from Dan Bailey, the Blue Star's first head chef, and because he could list the five mother sauces: béchamel, veloute, hollandaise, espagnole, and tomato sauce, James was offered a job at the Blue Star. After eight months as the sous chef, he became the head chef. That was in 1997.

For the past nine years, James has treated diners with his imaginative preparations. He has taken a few breaks from the restaurant, but his inspiration, creativity, and insistence on excellence set the standard for Blue Star fare.

The Owner

At age 14, Joseph E. Coleman, Jr. knew he wanted to own a restaurant. That year, he took his first restaurant job, working for Sonny Paine at the Crazy Cajun in Seabrook, Texas. He bussed tables, washed dishes, and shucked oysters. He loved the high energy of the restaurant business and of all the people who work in it. Joe came to Colorado Springs in 1989 because he wanted to be a chef at The Broadmoor. They hired him as a bellman instead. They fired him, too, but while he was there, he learned lasting lessons about customer service. For the next few years, he worked for several restaurants in Colorado Springs, including helping to open Wooglin's Deli and helping to reopen Poor Richard's as a pizzeria in 1992.

When Coleman opened the Blue Star 1995, he wanted to try out some ideas. He wanted co-workers to collaborate to improve the food and service at a fine restaurant. He wanted to give everyone room to better their skills and talents, to learn through successes and mistakes. He wanted to hire people who added a special touch to their part of the restaurant, be it bussing tables or preparing desserts. He also wanted a restaurant where anyone could walk in and feel completely comfortable, and where every customer is treated with the same high level of respect and service.

So far the experiments are working. He has attracted kitchen and serving staffs that share his commitment to high quality and creativity, and The Blue Star has hundreds of loyal customers. The Blue Star will always be a work in progress; that's Joe's nature.

The Writer

Molly Wingate is a writer who loves to cook and eat great food, so creating cookbooks was a natural. She started learning from James Davis when she kept asking him about the ingredients in dishes she ate at The Blue Star. When looking for a career change and thinking of culinary school, she talked her way into The Blue Star kitchen to watch, to learn, and to mash a remarkable number of red potatoes. She learned that she didn't want to go to culinary school, but she did want to create a Blue Star cookbook some day, so that ordinary people could learn to make this extraordinary food.

The Wine Guy

Drew Robinson is the voice of our wine pairings. Currently a sales representative and wine consultant for the wine distributor Grand Vin, Drew has 20 years of professional wine drinking/pairing/serving experience in several restaurants. He was the sommelier and bar manager at The Blue Star for five years. When he heard we wanted wine pairings for this cookbook, he pitched right in.

Drew Robinson, our wine guy.

The Beer Guy

Mike Bristol pushed us to think beyond wine for fine dining. An award-winning brewer and founder of Bristol Brewing Company, his experience, knowledge, and ability to argue got us thinking about beer pairings. Mike opened his brewery in 1994. He helped Joe construct The Blue Star's original beer list and remains an avid fan, friend, and next-door neighbor of The Blue Star.

Don Goede, Simpsonized.

The Designer and Photographer

Don Goede brings ten years of publishing experience to *The Blue Star Cookbook*. He has recently returned to the Colorado Springs area from New York City, and James W. Davis, Jr. is his favorite chef.

History of The Blue Star

The Blue Star opened in 1995 at 2802 West Colorado Avenue, in Colorado Springs, the brain child of Joseph Coleman, Jr. He assembled a cooking and serving staff that shared his unrelenting commitment to elegant, not stuffy, dining, and to attentive, not obsequious, service. The Blue Star's cuisine is influenced by Mediterranean and Pacific Rim cuisine. From the very start, the menu changed weekly, thus creating an atmosphere where its chefs invent, explore, and create. When asked, Coleman described the menu as schizophrenic. Diners came to see what the chefs were doing this week, not to eat the same dish they had a week or two ago.

The ever-changing menu remained the hallmark of The Blue Star when it moved in 1998 to 1645 South Tejon Street, next to the Bristol Brewery. The move demonstrated that The Blue Star had beaten the odds. It was a new restaurant with fresh ideas about food and service, and it was succeeding. With its own building, The Blue Star could define and secure its own destiny without the influence of others.

At 1645 South Tejon, The Blue Star has continued its evolution. In mid 2005, the staff wanted to see if they could raise the bar on the quality of the food by changing the menu less often, perhaps monthly, while still bringing new foods, new preparations, and fresh combinations to the table. The bar now offers customers opportunities to expand their palates through innovative wine tastings. The very knowledgeable serving staff strives to discover ways to make each visit to the restaurant an utter pleasure. The Blue Star tries never to rest on its laurels.

2802 West Colorado, before it became The Blue Star.

Chefs Dave and Dan outside the original Blue Star.

Eric Verlo

Most of The Blue Star staff, 1997.

Most of The Blue Star staff, 2005.

Tapas

Smoked Salmon Brie en Croûte

Stuffed Prince Edward Island Mussels

Thai Shrimp Cakes and Table Sauce

Coconut Peanut Shrimp Satay

Cheese Stuffed Poblano Pepper Wraps (vegetarian)

Athena's Goat Cheese Terrine (vegetarian)

Cuban Beef on Sugar Cane Skewers

Mojo Marinated Chicken Quesadillas

Smoked Salmon Brie en Croûte

This is a favorite tapa that has been with The Blue Star almost from the beginning. Inside a crisp, brown puff pastry, the brie, salmon and herbs combine for a full flavor and creamy texture. It is easy and can be prepared in advance. It is a wonderful treat to have in the freezer for those evenings after a day when nothing went right; a little salmon and brie can change the mood. Get ready for the raves.

Time:
1 hour 10 minutes
(including 30 minutes
of freezer time)
Equipment:
Pastry brush

SERVES 4

1/2 pound cold smoked, Nova Scotia-style salmon
2 tablespoons fresh parsley
1/2 teaspoon fresh thyme
1 tablespoon fresh chives
1 tablespoon olive oil
a dash of salt and pepper
1 pound round brie (4" in diameter and about 1" thick)
1 sheet commercial puff pastry
1 egg
1 tablespoon water

Toss the salmon with the oil and herbs. Halve the brie horizontally and sandwich the salmon mixture between the layers. Cut the brie and salmon sandwich into quarter wedges. Cut the puff pastry in 4 squares that are 4" X 4". Place a wedge of the brie in the middle of each piece of pastry.

In a separate bowl, whisk together the egg and water to make an egg wash. Seal the edges of the pastry around the brie, crimping the edges on the bottom side so the top of the tapa will be smooth. Brush with egg wash. Then place them in the freezer for 30 minutes to harden the brie. Bake in a 450° oven for 15 minutes or until brown.
Serve immediately or at room temperature. This recipe reheats in 7 minutes in a 350° oven.

See what you think of this equation: Pinot Noir + Salmon = Heaven
**Bouchard Pinot Noir Old Vines from Burgundy, France
Acacia, Pinot Noir from Carneros in California.**

Stuffed Prince Edward Island Mussels

For all those people who claim not to like mussels, this tapa will change their minds. If they won't even try these, well, that will leave more for the rest of us. The often-used phrase, "to die for," comes to mind. This tapa is pictured on page 66.

Time:
40 minutes,
if you have persillade
and hollandaise
prepared.
Add 40 minutes to
make persillade and
hollandaise.

20 whole cooked mussels,
    debearded
1/8 cup olive oil
1 tablespoon garlic, minced
1/4 cup yellow onion, finely diced
1 stalk celery, finely diced
2 tablespoons tasso
    (Cajun spiced ham)
3 green onion tops, chopped in
    1/4" rounds

1 sprig fresh thyme
    (1/2 teaspoon dried thyme)
1 tablespoon fresh parsley
    (2 teaspoons dried parsley)
splash of white wine
2 tablespoons bread crumbs
1 tablespoon butter, melted
salt and pepper to taste
1/2 cup persillade (p. 40)
1 cup James Davis's Hollandaise (p. 39)

Preheat oven to 350°.

Heat the oil pretty hot, but not smoking hot, and add the garlic to lightly toast it. The oil should foam a bit and the garlic will turn golden brown in a few seconds.* Immediately add yellow onion, celery, and tasso ham; turn the heat down to medium. Cook until the onions are translucent. Chop up the mussels and add them to the sauté. Add the onion tops, thyme, and parsley. Take the pan off the heat, add a splash of white wine, bread crumbs, and butter. Salt and pepper to taste.

Stuff the mussel shells with about a tablespoon each of this mixture; pack them tightly.

Sprinkle 1/2 teaspoon of persillade on each stuffed shell and place in oven for 5-7 minutes, until the persillade browns. You can also put them under a broiler, if you wish. Remove from oven, place 5 mussels on each plate, and drizzle each plate with 1/2 cup of James Davis's Hollandaise. Serve immediately.

*Chef's note: At the point that you have toasted the garlic in olive oil, you could strain out and you would have garlic-infused oil. Garlic-infused oil is great for dipping.

Mussels cry out for a crisp, high-acidity wine.
Geisen, Sauvignon Blanc from New Zealand
Condes de Albarei, Albariño from Spain

Thai Shrimp Cakes
and Table Sauce

Time: 30 minutes
Equipment: Hand grinder

These shrimp cakes start out as a gooey mess, and they transform into crispy-on-the-outside, moist-on-the-inside tasty treats. The Asian flavors of ginger and Kaffir lime leave sparkle on your palate. The light Thai table sauce on the next page provides a sweet and sour finish. This tapa is a little difficult, but the results are wonderful.

SERVES 4

Shrimp Cakes

1-1/4 pounds ground shrimp
2 garlic cloves, chopped
1-1/2 teaspoons crushed red pepper
3/4 teaspoon salt
3/4 teaspoon white pepper
1 tablespoon fresh ginger, chopped
1-1/2 teaspoons Kaffir lime leaves, very finely chopped
1 teaspoon cornstarch
2 green onions, chopped
2 egg whites, whipped to a medium peak
1 cup plain bread crumbs
6 tablespoons oil

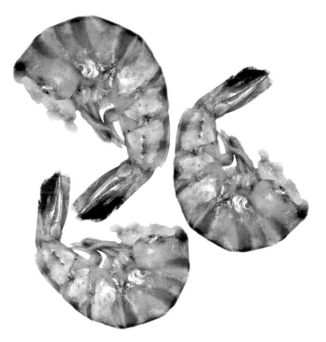

Shrimp

Time: 10 minutes
Makes 2-1/2 cups

Thai Table Sauce

1/4 cup nam pla (fish sauce)
1 cup hot water
2 cloves of garlic, crushed
1 teaspoon crushed red pepper

3/4 cup granulated sugar
1 teaspoon Karo syrup
3/4 cup fresh lime juice
   (about 2 limes)

Preheat oven to 350°.

Grind up the shrimp in a food processor—you'll get a shiny, sticky mess.

In a separate bowl, combine the garlic, crushed red pepper, salt, white pepper, ginger, and Kaffir lime leaves. Mix into shrimp.

Using your hands, mix in cornstarch and green onions. Then fold in egg whites, using your hands. Make palm-sized cakes. They will still be gooey.

Spread bread crumbs in a pie plate or flat plate. Plop the cakes in the bread crumbs and sprinkle bread crumbs on top.

Heat oil in sauté pan and pan fry the shrimp cakes for 1 minute a side. Then place in the oven, pan and all, for 6 to 8 minutes to complete cooking.

While the cakes are baking, make the sauce. Combine all the sauce ingredients in a bowl and stir.

Serve the shrimp cakes on a bed of greens with the table sauce on the side.

Belgian Golden Ale
This Belgian style has a dry, effervescent fruitiness, resulting from secondary fermentation in the bottle and its unique yeast strain. The zippy carbonation and clean hop bitterness scrub the palate between bites, allowing a sensational interplay of flavors from the spices, shrimp and hops. Pour it into a flute – who needs champagne?
Pranqster Belgian style Golden Ale, North Coast Brewing, California
La Chouffe – Brasserie D'Achouffe, Belgium

Coconut Peanut Shrimp Satay

The sweet and tangy sauce used in this recipe is perfect for Asian-influenced grilling. It can quickly become a house favorite. You can use it to marinate shrimp, fish, or fowl and then finish the dish using the sauce again.

Time: 30 minutes
Equipment: Skewers

SERVES 4

1 cup unsalted, shelled, roasted peanuts
1 cup sweet cream of coco
1 teaspoon tumeric
juice of one lime
1 tablespoon tamarind paste
1/2 teaspoon sambal or srirachi paste
salt to taste (adjust to salt in peanuts)
2 pounds large shrimp, shelled and deveined

Chef's notes: Use the excess cream of coco for a frozen piña colada while prepping the rest of your dinner! And save those shrimp shells to make shrimp essence (p. 32).

Place can of sweet cream of coco in a pan of warm water to make easier to empty the can. Then empty the can in a sauce pot and heat it to a boil. Add tumeric, lime juice, tamarind paste, and sambal or srirachi paste. Let mixture cool. Pour mixture into blender and add peanuts. Mix at a medium speed until smooth. Add salt to taste. Makes 2 cups of sauce.

Distribute the shrimp over 8 skewers. Pour half of the sauce on skewered shrimp and rub evenly before grilling. You will serve the other half of the sauce with the skewers, so be careful to not contaminate it with raw shrimp.

Grill shrimp until opaque – the amount of time depends on the heat of your grill. To serve as a tapa, place two skewers on each plate with a small dish of sauce. Garnish with cilantro. To serve as an entrée, add rice and steamed veggies.

Tough to match all the flavors of nuts, spice, and sweet, but try a good sherry. **Dios Baco Fino from Spain,** served slightly chilled. Fino is one of the lighter sherries, and a bit drier than the more common cream sherries. Don't be tempted by the cooking sherries you see on the bottom shelf at the liquor store.

Cheese Stuffed Poblano Pepper Wraps

We wrap the peppers in egg roll wrappers instead of dipping them in batter to make sure they are crunchy on the outside and gooey on the inside. Diners enjoy how the cheese mellows the heat of the poblanos. This tapa can be prepared in advance and cooked at the last minute.

Time: 45 minutes
Equipment:
Grill or gas burner
Small whisk
Brush

SERVES 4

10 fresh poblano peppers
1-3/4 cups queso blanco
1/2 cup pepper jack cheese
Salt and pepper to taste
1 egg
1/2 cup water

10 egg roll wrappers
1/2 cup corn starch
1/4 cup cooking oil
   (canola, vegetable or
   peanut)

The first step is to roast and peel the peppers. Put the peppers on a grill or hold them over a gas burner with a long-handled fork. Cook until the skin chars all over. Put the hot peppers in a plastic bag (or other airtight container) to sweat and cool them. When you can handle them, slide the skins off the peppers. Pull off the tops, remove the seeds, and make a slice the length of each pepper so it can be spread flat.

While the peppers are cooling, mix the cheeses together and salt and pepper to taste. Also make an egg wash by whisking together the egg and the water in a separate bowl.

When the peppers are peeled, you are ready to stuff them. Spread out one egg roll wrapper and brush it lightly with the egg wash. Place an open pepper in the middle of the wrap and fill the pepper with enough cheese so that you can fold the pepper closed. Close the pepper and fold diagonal corners of the wrapper over the pepper. Then roll the wrapper around the pepper like an egg roll. Roll the whole thing in corn starch to coat. Repeat for each pepper.
You can store these wraps up to three days.

To cook, heat oil in a frying pan and sauté the stuffed pepper wraps until the outside is golden brown, about 4 minutes depending on how hot your stove is. Serve immediately. You'll have two wraps per serving with two extras for your guests to arm-wrestle over.

Sparkling wine to contrast the spice.
Seaview Brut from Australia
Tattinger, La Francaise from France

Athena's Goat Cheese Terrine

The ingredients for this Greek-inspired tapa are divine. It is a bit difficult to create this five-layered terrine, but the results are beautiful and delicious. We mix the goat cheese with a little cream cheese to make the cheese layer a bit more creamy and pliable.

Time:
one hour prepping,
one hour in
the refrigerator
Equipment:
Muffin tins

SERVES
4

4 teaspoons extra virgin olive oil
1 tablespoon dried basil
2 tablespoons dried oregano
1 tablespoon dried thyme
2/3 cup goat cheese, French-style chèvre
1/4 cup cream cheese

1/2 cup sun dried tomatoes
 packed in oil, drained
2/3 cup calamata olives, pitted
2/3 cup canned artichoke hearts,
 quartered and squeezed as dry as possible

Chef's note: The drier the artichokes, the better the terrine will hold together.

First, prepare the muffin tins. The muffin tins will serve as the mold for each terrine. The difficulty making a terrine isn't so much putting the ingredients in, but getting them out as a neat package. You have two choices for preparing the tins: (1) generously oil each muffin cup with olive oil or (2) line each with plastic wrap. It's your call.

Now for the ingredients. Blend the herbs and coat the bottom of four prepared muffin cups (this is a little harder to do with the plastic wrap liners). Blend the goat cheese and cream cheese. Purée the vegetables separately. The olives will make a thin paste, the sun dried tomatoes will be a thick paste, and the artichoke quarters will be almost dry.

Dampen your hands with water. With 2 tablespoons of the cheese mixture, form a patty of cream cheese the diameter of the muffin cups and 1/4 inch thick or less. Press one patty in the bottom of each muffin cup. Make sure the each layer goes all the way to the edge. The next layer is artichoke purée, one-quarter of purée for each terrine. Then another layer of cheese. Then a layer of sun dried tomato purée, one-quarter of the purée for each terrine, and another layer of cheese. Finish with a layer of puréed olives, again one-quarter for each terrine. Cover the terrines and refrigerate for 45 minutes to an hour.

To remove the terrines from oiled tins, run a knife along the circumference of each cup, place a cookie sheet on top of the muffin tin, and them flip the tin over, cookie sheet and all, and gently tap each inverted cup. To remove the terrines from plastic wrap-lined cups, gently tug at the plastic wrap to loosen them. Place a cookie sheet on top of the muffin tin and flip over the tin and sheet together. Gently tap the inverted cups. Serve with sliced ciabatta, a flat Italian bread.

This needs something crisp to balance out the tomato, olive and rich cheese.
Pascal Jolivet, Sancerre from Loire Valley, France
Napa Wine Company, Sauvignon Blanc from Napa

Cuban Beef on Sugar Cane Skewers

The sugar cane swizzle sticks add to the Caribbean flair of this tapa. You will start by making mojo sauce, a Cuban barbecue sauce, marinade, and dipping sauce that uses a little fruit, garlic, and spice to give some zip to grilled meat. You can marinate the meat well in advance of serving and cook it at the last minute. See picture on page 69. You can also use the mojo sauce with any grilled meat and in Mojo Marinated Chicken Quesadillas (p. 10).

Time: 30 minutes
cooking, 1 hour
marinating (at least)

**Sauce makes
1 cup**

SERVES
4

Mojo Sauce
1/2 cup olive oil
1/4 onion, sliced
1 tablespoon garlic, chopped
1/4 cup mango purée
1/4 cup white wine
1 tablespoon oregano

1 teaspoon ground cumin
1 lime, juiced
salt and black pepper to taste

1-1/2 lbs. of tri-tips cut into 1" cubes
4 sugar cane sticks, split lengthwise
       into 1/4" diameter skewers;
       make a point on one end.

Chef's note: Instead of tri-tips, you can use scraps from a tenderloin, tender sirloin, New York strip or filet mignon. You can also use pork loin or tenderloin. Feel free to add peppers and onions to your skewers.

In a small sauce pan, heat the oil to warm and add all the ingredients except the meat and sugar cane. Cook until the onions are translucent. You don't want the marinade to cook the meat, so chill the sauce in the refrigerator. Use a shallow dish or cookie sheet to speed the process along.

Cut meat into cubes and marinate in mojo sauce for at least an hour. Skewer the beef pieces on cane sticks. Grill to your preference, but not for more than a few minutes. The amount of time will depend on how hot your grill is. Serve as an entrée with green rice (p. 77) and Regina's Black Beans (p. 79).

A good wine to go with barbecue is **Zinfandel**, the red stuff.
Renwood, the Sierra Series can be found for less than $12.
Seghesio Old Vine, or one of **Renwood's, Ridge or Rosenblum** single
vineyard **Zinfandels** for a bit more spice.

Mojo Marinated Chicken Quesadillas

A tasty tapa or light lunch. These quesadillas stand out with the full flavors of mojo sauce and pesto. Instead of chicken, you can also use pork loin or beef strips in this recipe.

2 chicken breasts, julienned
1 cup mojo sauce (p. 9)
2 tablespoons sun dried
    tomato pesto (p. 37)
8 6-inch corn tortillas

2 cups crumbled queso blanco
    (you can also grate
    pepper jack or
    Monterey jack cheese)
8 sprigs of cilantro
2 tablespoons oil

Time: 50 minutes if you have mojo sauce & sun-dried tomato pesto on hand
Add 30 minutes to make and cool the mojo sauce.
The pesto takes 25 minutes; you can make it while the chicken is marinating.

Marinate chicken in mojo sauce for 30 minutes. This could be the time to make the pesto.

Cook the chicken and the mojo sauce in a saucepan over medium heat until chicken is done, about 15 minutes. The cooked chicken should shred a bit.

Spread 1-1/2 teaspoons of sun dried tomato pesto on each of 4 tortillas. Sprinkle with 1/2 cup of crumbled cheese and distribute the chicken and mojo evenly over the 4 tortillas. Place 2 sprigs of cilantro on each and top with a second corn tortilla.

Heat oil in pan and cook the quesadillas 1-2 minutes and then flip them for another 1-2 minutes. Cook until the tortillas are lightly browned on edges. You can also grill the quesadillas; 45 seconds to 2 minutes a side.

Cut the quesadillas in quarters and place on a plate. If you would like to make this an entrée, serve with Fruity Guacamole (p. 78), Corn Confetti (p. 78), and Pico de Gallo (p. 80).

SERVES 4

Bavarian Wheat Beer: A cloudy, refreshing style with hints of banana, clove and green apples. The carbonation and acidity of this beer cut through the oils of the pesto, while the malt sweetness tempers the spice and allows the flavors to meld. The earthy character of the beer matches extremely well with the cilantro, mojo sauce and corn tortillas.

Tabernash Weiss – Left Hand/Tabernash Brewery, Colorado
Schneider Weiss – G. Schneider & Sohn, Germany

Salads

Tahini Vinaigrette over Spinach with
Grilled Vidalia Onions and Toasted Pine Nuts (vegan)

Red Leaf Lettuce and Asparagus Bundles
with Raspberry Vinaigrette (vegan)

Institutional Salad (vegetarian)

Company Salad (vegetarian)

Mixed Greens with Dried Fruit Cambozola Roulade,
Rhubarb Compote, and Port Vinaigrette (vegetarian)

Bocconcini Caprese Salad (vegetarian)

Smoked Salmon and Black Pepper Strawberries on Spinach

Warm Cabbage with Prosciutto Vinaigrette

Herbed Crostini (vegetarian)

The Vinaigrettes

Tahini Vinaigrette over Spinach
with Grilled Vidalia Onions and Toasted Pine Nuts

This salad is rich in textures and flavors. It may look like a lot of work for the salad course, but the result is worth every minute. It can stand alone as a power lunch, or add a grilled chicken breast or shrimp for an entrée.

Time: 30 minutes
if you have
Bomb Sauce and Tahini
Vinaigrette on hand.
Add 20 minutes
to make Bomb Sauce
Add 15 minutes to
make the Tahini
Vinaigrette

3 tablespoons pine nuts
1 Vidalia onion, cut into
    3/4 inch vertical slices
1 tablespoon Bomb Sauce (p. 38)
1 teaspoon salt
2 ounces Tahini Vinaigrette (p. 24)
6 cups of fresh spinach

Toasted Pine Nuts

SERVES 4

In a 300° oven, toast the pine nuts for 7-8 minutes. Separate the onion slices into individual rings to get about 20 rings, enough for five servings. Rub Bomb Sauce on the rings, sprinkle with salt and grill or sauté until tender, yet still formed in a ring. In a bowl, toss together the spinach and Tahini Vinaigrette. Top the greens with the grilled onions. Sprinkle with toasted pine nuts.

Chef's note: You can also use red onions if Vidalias are out of season.

Matching wine with vinegar-based dressings is tricky, so let's focus on the nuttier flavors to match up with the tahini.
Preston Ranch Vineyards, Marsanne from Dry Creek Valley
Segura Viudas, Heredad Brut Reserva from Spain

Red Leaf Lettuce and Asparagus Bundles with Raspberry Vinaigrette

A colorful, tasty salad that is perfect any time of year, or when you can find asparagus, whichever comes first. The sweet and sour raspberry vinaigrette sets off the asparagus, which is tied up with a scallion. There is a color picture on page 67.

Time: 20 minutes,
if you have Raspberry
Vinaigrette
on hand.
Add 10 minutes to
make the dressing.

Equipment:
Steamer
Large bowl of water
with ice

**28 stalks of asparagus
6 scallions with greens,
about 6" long
12 nice, clean, red leaf
lettuce leaves
4 ounces Raspberry
Vinaigrette (p. 23)**

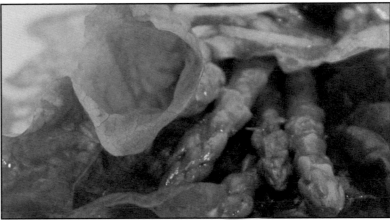
Close up of Red Leaf Lettuce and Asparagus Bundles

First, make an ice bath so you are ready for the asparagus and scallions. Steam the asparagus for 5 minutes, until tender. Shock in an ice bath immediately. Steam the scallion greens for 2 minutes and shock in ice bath.

The picture on page 67 will help as you assemble the bundles. For each bundle, you will need 3 leaves of lettuce, 7 stalks of asparagus, and 1 scallion. Because the scallions sometimes tear, we've asked you to blanch 2 extra. Place 2 lettuce leaves on the plate with the stalks overlapping and the ruffled edges pointing in opposite directions. Place the asparagus stalks on the lettuce, 3 on one leaf and 4 on the other, with their stalks in the middle and their heads pointing out. Tear off the ruffled, red half of the third leaf of lettuce. Wrap it around the middle of the asparagus and lettuce like a belt; tie the scallion around it to hold it together. Make 4 bundles, and put one on each plate.

Drizzle each bundle with 1 ounce of Raspberry Vinaigrette.

Chef's note: You can garnish this salad with fresh raspberries.

Rose should be served to match up with the raspberries.
Renwood Syrah Rose from Amador County
Tablas Creek Rosé from Paso Robles, California

Institutional Salad

When you have a refrigerator shelf full of almost empty bottles of condiments, this is the salad to make. This salad got its name from trying to make good use of little amounts of leftover condiments in an institutional or commercial kitchen.

Time: 20 minutes, if you already have herbed crostini Add 20 minutes to make the crostini

Dressing makes 2 cups.

Dressing
2 teaspoons Dijon mustard
1 egg yolk
1-1/2 cups of olive oil
1-1/2 teaspoons chopped garlic
1/2 shallot, finely diced
1-1/2 teaspoons parsley, chopped
salt and pepper to taste
1-1/2 teaspoons lemon juice
1-1/2 teaspoons sherry
2 teaspoons Worcestershire sauce
A dash of ketchup, A-1 Steak
    sauce, or anything like that
    (use as many as you wish).

2 tablespoons red wine vinegar

Salad
3 cups of 1" romaine squares
1 tomato diced
1/2 cup pitted calamata olives
1/4 cup asiago or parmesan
    cheese, grated
12 slices herbed crostini (p. 21)

SERVES 4

To make the dressing, blend the mustard and egg yolks with a whisk or balloon whisk. Then very, very slowly add olive oil in a thin stream until it is completely mixed (emulsified) and a little frothy; continue until all the oil is incorporated. Then add all the other dressing ingredients.

In a salad bowl, combine romaine, tomato, olives, and cheese. Toss with dressing. Divide over 4 plates. Top each salad with 3 crostini. This can be augmented with grilled chicken or shrimp to make a lovely lunch.

Chef's note: A balloon whisk is lighter and whips more air in a mixture, making this particular dressing much easier to prepare.

Guerrieri-Rizzardi, Soave Classico (Soave is usually considered inferior, but get a Classico and taste the difference)
Spring Mountain, Sauvignon Blanc from Napa

Company Salad

A hearty salad that can stand alone as lunch, the Company Salad uses the Sun Dried Tomato Pesto recipe in this book and fresh spinach. It is healthful, yummy, and lovely. Feel free to add some grilled chicken to make a substantial meal of it.

Time:
20 minutes,
if the pesto is
already made.
Add 20 minutes to
make the pesto.
Equipment:
zester

SERVES 4

6 cups fresh spinach
4 tablespoons sun dried tomato pesto (p. 37)
1 shallot, finely sliced in rings
zest of one organic lemon
20 curls of shaved reggiano parmigiano

In a bowl, sprinkle the spinach with the pesto and hand toss without bruising the leaves. Divide the spinach and shallot rings over four plates. Sprinkle 1/4 of the lemon zest on each serving. Top with 5 cheese curls.

Chef's note: Parmesan cheese works, too.

A rosé will hold up nicely to all the rich ingredients here.
Toad Hollow Pinot Noir Rosé from Sonoma, California
Zaca Mesa Rosé from Santa Ynez Valley

Mixed Greens with Dried Fruit Cambozola
Roulade, Rhubarb Compote, and Currant Port Vinaigrette

What a wonderful plateful of flavors and contrasts! The rich, triple cream of cambozola cheese surrounds the bits of dried fruit so that the flavors and textures commingle. This alchemy complements the bright flavors of the rhubarb compote and mixed greens. This recipe has several individual preparations, so you can do them at the same time or space them over a day or two. See picture on page 66.

Time:
1-1/2 to 2 hours
Equipment:
parchment paper

The Salad
4 cups mixed greens
1 cup Currant Port
    Vinaigrette (p. 23)
1/2 cup walnuts

Dried Fruit Cambozola
1/2 cup of mixed dried fruit*
1/2 pound of cambozola cheese

*We suggest cherries, apricots, figs, currants, and raisins.
Do not use pineapple, mango, or other tropical fruit.

SERVES 4

Dice the fruit until the pieces are smaller than 1/2 inch. Peel the cambozola and place in a mixing bowl. Add the fruit and completely combine. Place a 12-inch piece of parchment paper on a countertop and put the cheese and fruit mixture on top. Shape the mixture into a log about 1-1/2 inch in diameter. Fold the parchment over the roll so that the roll is surrounded by parchment. Place the square edge of a baking sheet along the edge of the covered log and use the pan to push the log firmly into the parchment to make a uniform roundness. Roll up the log and wrap in plastic wrap. Refrigerate for at least 30 minutes. To serve, remove parchment and slice the roll.

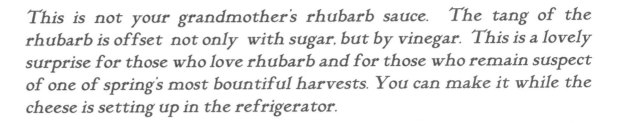

Rhubarb Compote

This is not your grandmother's rhubarb sauce. The tang of the rhubarb is offset not only with sugar, but by vinegar. This is a lovely surprise for those who love rhubarb and for those who remain suspect of one of spring's most bountiful harvests. You can make it while the cheese is setting up in the refrigerator.

Time:
20 minutes
plus 30 minutes
in the
refrigerator

1/4 cup olive oil

2 cups rhubarb, cut into 1/8" slices

1/3 cup shallots, minced

1/4 cup sugar

Salt and pepper to taste

1 tablespoon apple cider vinegar

1/3 bunch of Italian parsley, rough chopped

In a medium saucepan, heat the oil and sauté the shallots. Add the sliced rhubarb and continue the sauté until the rhubarb is a little limp. The mixture will get reddish. Mix in the sugar, salt, and pepper. Then add the apple cider vinegar. Deglaze the pan and turn off the heat. Add the parsley and stir. Spread the mixture in a shallow pan to cool.

Make the Currant Port Vinaigrette (p. 23) while the rhubarb is cooling. It takes about 35 minutes.

To serve this salad, put 1 cup of greens on each plate and drizzle with 2 ounces of Currant Port Vinaigrette. Put three 1/4-inch slices of the cambozola roulade on the greens and spoon 1/2 cup of rhubarb compote on top. Garnish with walnuts.

Chef's note: Roulade can be served on its own as a cheese course with a nice glass of tawny port. You can also spread this roulade on crackers for an appetizer. If kept refrigerated, it will last a few weeks and still taste great. Just keep it around; you'll think of excuses to devour it.

A light red will match up well with the dried fruits and rhubarb.
Gagliardo Barbera d'Alba from Italy
Ca' del Solo, Charbono, "La Farfalla," California

Bocconcini Caprese Salad

This beautiful and textured rendition of an Italian favorite uses little tomatoes and little mozzarella balls, bocconcini. A quick and easy salad, it complements more complicated entrées and is very nice with summer meat dishes. Be sure to make enough for second helpings. See the picture on page 70.

Time:
20 minutes

Cherry Tomatos

1 pint cherry tomatoes, halved
1-1/2 cups baby mozzarella balls (bocconcini)
2 tablespoons white balsamic vinegar
2 tablespoons olive oil
freshly ground, black pepper to taste
1/8 teaspoon crushed red peppers
kosher salt to taste
12 large fresh basil leaves
2 cups mixed greens

SERVES 4

Combine tomatoes, bocconcini, vinegar, olive oil, black pepper, crushed red peppers, and kosher salt; toss very gently. Stack the basil leaves and roll together lengthwise. Make the tiniest slices you can to produce ribbons (or chiffonade) of basil, see picture on page 107. Add basil on top. Serve on mixed greens. Serves 4.

Chef's Note: Whole baby heirloom or tear drop tomatoes are great in this salad, too.

With tomatoes and mozzarella, what else but an Italian?
Zenato Pinot Grigio
Luna Pinot Grigio from California
(one of the best examples of a "New World" Pinot)

Smoked Salmon
and Black Pepper Strawberries on Spinach

Time:
40 minutes

The perfect summer salad entrée for lunch or dinner. The tartness of the salmon along with the sweet/hot of the marinated strawberries fills your mouth with flavors while the fresh spinach provides crunch to offset the soft textures. The pink, red, and green colors make this a beauty to serve.

SERVES
4

- 1 tablespoon black peppercorns
- 1/4 cup white balsamic vinegar
- salt to taste
- 2 cups fresh or frozen strawberries, thinly sliced
- 4 tablespoons extra virgin olive oil
- 1 quart fresh spinach

- 8 ounces smoked salmon
- 1 shallot, thinly sliced
- 4 tablespoons carrot curls
- 4 more tablespoons extra virgin olive oil

Use a pepper grinder with a large grind or use a knife to chop up the black pepper (this pepper preparation is called mignonette). Combine vinegar, black pepper, and salt; submerge the strawberry slices in the liquid. Cover and refrigerate for at least 30 minutes.

Drain the strawberries; reserve the liquid. Blend the liquid from the strawberries with 4 tablespoons of olive oil and pour over the spinach. Toss. Then distribute the spinach over four plates, top with the marinated strawberries, and place 2 ounces of salmon on each salad.

Using a vegetable peeler, shave strips 1/8" thick off a carrot to make 1 inch curls. Garnish the salad with shallot slices and carrot curls. Drizzle each salad with another tablespoon of olive oil.

Chef's note: You can use mixed greens instead of spinach if you prefer. You can also grill fresh salmon instead of using smoked salmon.

We need lighter reds with salmon; this one needs to be a bit fruitier to match with the strawberries.
Louis Jadot, Beaujolais from France
Saintsbury "Garnet" Pinot Noir from California

Warm Cabbage
with Prosciutto Vinaigrette

The warm colors and temperature make this a perfect winter salad, but it is also an ample lunch any time. Just try it; you'll love it. See a color picture on page 66.

Time:
20 minutes
for the salad, add
30 minutes
to make the dressing

SERVES
4

2 tablespoons salad or olive oil
1/2 small head of red cabbage, julienned
salt and pepper to taste
8 ounces Prosciutto Vinaigrette (p. 22)
4 tablespoons diced tomatoes
4 teaspoons crumbled feta
4 slices of prosciutto, thinly sliced

Close up of Warm Cabbage with Prosciutto Vinaigrette

Sauté cabbage in oil until hot and still a little crunchy. Add salt and pepper. Mix in prosciutto vinaigrette, toss and heat for 2 or 3 minutes. Divide salad over four plates and top each with a tablespoon of chopped tomatoes and a teaspoon of crumbled feta. Garnish with a folded piece of prosciutto.

A bit of red wine here, but not too heavy.
Georges DuBoeuf, Morgon region of Beaujolais, Jean Descombes
Produttori del Barbaresco, Barbaresco, from Langhe, Italy

Herbed Crostini

Homemade croutons are infinitely tastier than the store-bought ones and are very easy to make. We include this recipe to top off Swiss Onion Soup (p. 26), Institutional Salad (p. 14) and as a vehicle for Sun Dried Tomato Pesto (p. 37). After you make these crostini, you may have to hide them until you want to serve them because everyone likes to snack on them.

Time:
20 minutes
Makes: 20-24 slices

Italian Bread

1 medium loaf of French or
      Italian bread, white or wheat
1/4 cup olive oil
Garlic salt to taste
2 tablespoons dried oregano

Preheat oven to 350°.

Slice bread into 1/2" thick rounds and place on baking sheet. Brush with olive oil but do not soak. Evenly sprinkle garlic salt and oregano on slices. Place in preheated oven for 10-12 minutes, until the bread is very lightly toasted.

Chef's note: If you have a squeeze bottle with a small nozzle on it, you can use it to squirt the oil.

The Vinaigrettes

Dressings can make or break a salad. Here are the vinaigrette dressings mentioned in this book along with a bonus recipe. This collection could signal the end of commercial vinaigrettes in your refrigerator.

Oil and Vinegar

Prosciutto Vinaigrette

You might wonder about prosciutto in a salad dressing. Where are the sweet raspberries or the balsamic vinegar? Even James Davis has a hard time keeping a straight face when describing this dressing for Warm Cabbage with Prosciutto Vinaigrette (p. 20).

Time:
30 minutes
(if you
already
have
chicken
stock)

Makes 1 cup

1/4 pound prosciutto or
    serrano ham,
    thinly sliced
1/2 cup extra virgin
    olive oil
1/2 large yellow onion,
    julienned
2 tablespoons garlic,
    chopped
1/4 cup sugar
1/2 cup chicken stock
    (p.33)

1 cup apple cider
    vinegar
2 tablespoons Dijon
    mustard
2 tablespoons Italian
    parsley, chopped
Salt and black pepper
    to taste

Sauté the prosciutto in 1/4 cup of oil until crispy. Add onions and garlic, sauté until the onions are translucent. Remove from pan and reserve.

In a saucepan, combine the sugar, chicken stock, apple cider vinegar, and the prosciutto mixture. Boil until it is reduced by 2/3 to 3/4, however you like it. The dressing should not be too heavy. Add Dijon mustard. Purée the reduced mixture while adding remaining 1/4 cup of olive oil. Blend in with parsley, salt, and pepper.

Raspberry Vinaigrette

★ ★

*A perfect dressing for simple green
salads; this dressing is light and flavorful.
We use it with Red Leaf Lettuce and
Asparagus Bundles with Raspberry
Vinaigrette (p. 13).*

Time:

10 minutes

**Makes 2
cups.**

Shallots

1/2 shallot, puréed or finely chopped
1/2 cup raspberry vinegar
1 tablespoon Dijon mustard
1/8 cup honey (to taste)
1/2 cup raspberry jam or preserves
1-1/2 cup olive oil or salad oil
salt and pepper to taste

Blend shallots, raspberry vinegar, mustard,
honey, and jam or preserves in a food processor or blender. Slowly add the oil into the
mixture. Salt and black pepper to taste.

Currant Port Vinaigrette

*We use this dressing as the finishing sauce for the recipe Mixed
Greens with Dried Fruit Cambozola Roulade, Rhubarb Compote
and Port Vinaigrette (p. 16).*

**Makes 2
cups**

1 cup tawny port
2 tablespoons dried currants (red, black, or yellow)
1/2 cup balsamic vinegar
1 shallot, minced
1 tablespoon fresh parsley, chopped
1-1/2 cup salad oil
salt and pepper to taste

Reduce port by three quarters in a small sauce
pan over a low heat, 20 minutes. Purée the
currants in the balsamic vinegar. Add port,
shallot, and parsley. Slowly add the oil into
the mixture. Salt and pepper to taste.

Tahini Vinaigrette

Time: 15 minutes

Makes 2 cups

This nutty-flavored dressing will soon become a household favorite. It can be used with almost any greens. It will make even iceberg taste new. We suggest you try it in the salad Tahini Vinaigrette over Spinach with Grilled Vidalia Onions and Toasted Pine Nuts (p. 12).

Garlic Bulbs

2 tablespoons whole grain mustard
1/4 cup honey
3 tablespoons tahini
1/2 teaspoon white pepper
salt to taste
1/2 cup red wine or champagne vinegar

juice of one lemon (1/8 to 1/4 cup)
3/4 cup water
2 garlic cloves, rough chopped
2 shallots, rough chopped
1 cup olive oil

Combine ingredients except the oil in a blender or food processor. Slowly add the oil and blend until emulsified.

Balsamic Vinaigrette

Time: 20 minutes

Makes 2 cups

This distinctly flavorful dressing is easy to make and keeps well in the refrigerator. If you add the oil using a food processor, it will not separate. We do not mention this dressing in other recipes, but we suggest you use it for any green salad including the Red Leaf Lettuce and Asparagus Bundles (p. 13).

1-1/2 teaspoons Dijon mustard
6 tablespoons balsamic vinegar
1/2 shallot, finely diced
1-1/2 teaspoons parsley, chopped
1-1/2 teaspoons fresh basil, chopped

1-1/2 cups of olive oil
salt and pepper to taste

Chef's note: If you would prefer a slightly sweeter vinaigrette, add honey to your sweet content.

Blend the mustard, vinegar, shallot, parsley, and basil with a whisk or balloon whisk. Then, using a food processor, very, very slowly add olive oil in a thin stream until it is completely mixed (emulsified); continue until all the oil is incorporated. Add salt and pepper to taste.

Soups, Stocks, Sauces, and Toppings

Swiss Onion Soup

Butternut Bisque (vegetarian)

Chicken Lime Tortilla Soup

Carrot Cumin Soup (vegetarian)

Jamaica Jerk Conch Chowder

Shrimp Essence

Chicken Stock

Vegetable Stock (vegan)

Veal Stock, Demi-glace, Glace de Viande

Mushroom Stock (vegan)

Sun Dried Tomato Pesto (vegetarian)

Chipotle Aioli (vegetarian)

Bomb Sauce (vegan)

James Davis's Hollandaise (vegetarian)

Persillade (vegan)

Warlock Onions (vegan)

Swiss Onion Soup

We can thank Lucas Callanan for bringing this soup down Ute Pass from Woodland Park's Swiss Chalet. The difference from French onion soup is that Swiss onion soup uses chicken stock, instead of beef, and Swiss onion soup has a thicker texture. This sweet, country-style soup is magnificent. I heard one diner exclaim, "I'd take a bath in this. Onions are good for the skin, right?"

Time: 1 hour if you have chicken stock and herbed crostini on hand.
Add 5 hours for chicken stock
Add 20 minutes for crostini

1 large yellow onion, julienned
8 tablespoons unsalted butter
2 teaspoons cracked black pepper
1/4 cup all purpose flour
4 cups chicken stock, cold (p.33)
Salt to taste

A few drops of mushroom soy sauce or Maggi sauce (optional)
4 herbed crostini (p. 21)
3/4 c. grated Gruyere or Emmenthaler cheese (optional)

SERVES 4

Melt butter in pot and add onions. Cook over a medium/low heat and caramelize the onions, about 20 minutes. Do not burn the onions. When the onions are goopy and a little brown, add pepper and flour. Stir until all the butter is absorbed and cook this roux until it smells nutty and is a little brown, 5-10 minutes.

This next step determines the texture of the soup – which should be smooth and velvety. Slowly add the cold chicken stock and stir constantly to remove any lumps of roux. Bring the soup up to temperature, but do not boil. Add salt to taste. If you wanted to finish this like the Swiss do, try adding a few drops of Maggi to it. We also like to finish the soup with a few drops of mushroom soy sauce.

Serve in 4 bowls. Place a crostini on the top of each and distribute the grated cheese over the bowls. Place under a hot broiler for 4 minutes, until the cheese melts and browns around the edges.

This dish has a bit of spice that would go along great with spicy **Gewurztraminer**.
Inexpensive and easy to find: **Trimbach, Alsace region of France**
A bit pricier but worth it: anything by **Zind-Humbrecht**, also from Alsace

Butternut Bisque

The warm yellow color, smooth texture, and great fragrance of this soup help explain why this recipe is often requested. This soup is perfect for a fall or winter lunch with a salad or as a first course. It is easy to prepare, and it will make your kitchen smell very inviting.

Time:
2 hours, 30
minutes active

SERVES 4

2 butternut squash
4 teaspoons butter
1/4 teaspoon of cinnamon
1/4 teaspoon of nutmeg
1/8 cup pine nuts

1-1/2 cups vegetable stock (p. 34)
2/3 cup heavy cream
salt and white pepper to taste
2 tablespoons oil
8 leaves of fresh sage

Chef's note: If you don't have vegetable stock on hand, you can make it while the squash is baking and cooling. Also, if you would like this to be a lighter soup, add milk in place of cream.

Preheat oven to 350°.

Halve the squash, scoop out the seeds. Place on a baking sheet skin side down. Place 1 teaspoon of butter and a dash of cinnamon and nutmeg in each half. Bake for one hour or until the pulp of the squash is soft. Let the squash cool so that you can handle it. While the squash is baking and cooling, toast the pine nuts in the oven for 5 or 6 minutes, until golden brown. You will have enough time to make the vegetable stock.

Scoop out the pulp from the skins of the squash and place in a large soup pot. Add the stock, stir, and boil for 5 minutes. Add heavy cream, salt, and pepper and mix with a blender at a medium speed until it is smooth. Keep the soup warm, but do not boil it once the cream is in.

In a sauté pan, heat the oil. Drop the sage leaves into the oil and step back because the oil tends to pop. When the leaves are dark green, remove them from the oil. Drain them on a paper towel.

Divide the soup over four bowls and garnish with toasted pine nuts and crumbled, fried sage leaves.

A good sherry should do nicely, matching the nuttiness and creaminess of the soup.
Any Fino or Amontillado

Chicken Lime Tortilla Soup

★ ★ ★

We thank Corey Wilson for this recipe which has all the basic flavors: sweet, sour, spicy, and salty. It will warm your palate and your stomach. It takes some time to make, but you will enjoy treating your diners to this artful and beautiful starter or entrée.

Time:
2 hours
if you have chicken stock and cooked chicken meat on hand.
Add 1-1/2 hours to roast a chicken.
Add 5 hours to make stock.
Equipment:
Very fine zester

Makes 6 bowls or 8 cups.

2 limes to zest
2 poblano peppers
4 corn tortillas
1 cup cooking oil, enough for
        1/2" in a large frying pan

1/4 pound bacon, minced
1-1/2 onions, medium diced
2 stalks of celery, sliced
1 carrot, halved lengthwise and
        sliced to create half moons
1-1/2 small red bell peppers,
        medium diced

2 tomatoes, seeded and diced
3 raw jalapeños, seeded and
        minced
2 tablespoons garlic, minced
3-1/2 teaspoons oregano
2-1/2 teaspoons cumin

1/4 cup white wine
3 quarts chicken stock (p. 33)

1 cup corn (fresh or frozen)
1/3 cup chopped corn tortillas
2-1/2 cups chicken meat, coarse
        chopped

2 tablespoons salt
2 tablespoons black pepper
juice from the 2 limes
        you zested

Garnish
1 pint sour cream
a small bunch of cilantro
        strip off the leaves
        and finely chop
white pepper to taste
salt to taste

First, we need to prepare some of the ingredients.

1. Make sure you have cooked chicken meat and chicken stock on hand. If not, roast a medium-sized chicken, remove the meat, and use these bones (along with others) to make stock (p. 33). You can also use commercial, low-salt stock or broth.

2. Using a fine zester, zest 2 limes, getting only the green of the lime. Spread the zest on a tray and let it dry out in a warm place such as an oven that has just been turned off.

3. Roast the poblano peppers. The point of this procedure is to remove the skins and seeds. Using a broiler, grill or gas burner, get the peppers hot (a little charring is fine). Then quickly cover the peppers so that they steam. A sealed plastic bag is perfect. After 20 minutes, you will be able to easily scrape the skins off the peppers with the edge of a knife and pull the seeds out. Chop.

4. Fry tortilla strips. Stack the four corn tortillas and cut into 1/2" strips. Remove the really short strips. Heat oil in frying pan and drop in the tortilla strips a few at a time. Stir to avoid burning. When the oil on the strips ceases to bubble, the strips are done. Drain in a bowl with a paper towel in it.

Now to the soup!

Render the minced bacon and add diced onions, celery, carrots and red bell pepper. Sauté the vegetables until they are soft and the onions just begin to take on an amber color – about 15 minutes. Add diced tomatoes and cook until the liquid of the tomatoes comes out. Add jalapeños and garlic and sauté for 5 minutes. It is important not to burn the peppers or garlic. Add the oregano and cumin. Add wine and deglaze the pot. Add chicken stock and boil (see chef's note). Turn down the stove and simmer the soup until all the ingredients are soft, about 15 minutes or longer if you have the time.

Add corn, chopped roasted poblanos, and boil soup. Add 1/3 cup chopped tortillas and boil until the tortillas dissolve. Be careful to stir the soup and scrape the bottom of the pot; it is easy to burn the soup once the tortillas are in. Add coarse chopped chicken meat. Heat until all ingredients are warm. The next step is to balance the acid and salt flavors in the soup. Start by adding one half of the lime juice, salt, and pepper. Add more of each until you like the taste.

To assemble for serving, combine the sour cream and cilantro in a separate bowl. Add salt and white pepper to taste. Put soup in cups or bowl. Put a dollop of sour cream mixture on each, add a small handful of fried tortilla strips and sprinkle with a few pinches of lime zest.

This recipe makes a bit extra, and you'll be glad you have it as the requests for seconds begin.

Chef's note: You may want to add more stock to increase the ratio of liquid to vegetables for a thinner soup or add more tortillas to make the soup thicker. People tend to like thicker soups in the winter and thinner ones in the summer.

Something with some citrus zip to go along with the lime.
Undurraga, Sauvignon Blanc from Chile
Morgadio, Albariño from the Rias Baixas region of northwestern Spain.

Carrot Cumin Soup

This thick soup surprises people with its earthy, spicy flavor. It is rich without being heavy and provides a great lunch on its own or as a complement to a sandwich or salad.

4 large carrots, chopped

6 tablespoons unsalted butter

3/4 gallon of water

1/2 cup mushroom stock, approximately (p. 37)

2-1/2 teaspoons whole cumin or 2 teaspoons of
    ground cumin

1 pinch of white pepper

salt to taste

Time:
1 hour
Equipment:
spice grinder
or mortar and pestle

Makes 6 cups or 4 bowls of soup

Boil chopped carrots and butter in water until very soft. Cover the pot to preserve the water while cooking. If you need to make the mushroom stock, you can do it while the carrots are cooking. Drain and purée the carrots. If the purée seems a bit dry, add a little of the water you cooked carrots in. Add mushroom stock until the soup is the desired consistency.

Toast the whole cumin in a dry sauté pan over a flame until the cumin gives off a perfume-like fragrance. Then grind the cumin in a spice mill or mortar and pestle.

Add cumin and white pepper; finish the purée. Adjust the cumin, pepper, and salt to suit your taste. Heat the soup to serve it warm.

Chef's note: You can substitute vegetable stock for mushroom stock, or you can use a commercial soup/stock base. Watch out for the salt in a commercial product; it can ruin the soup.

The viscous texture and mushroom stock call for something crisp, yet slightly earthy.
**Marqués de Cacéres, White Rioja from Spain
Guigal, Cotes du Rhone Rosé from France**

Jamaica Jerk Conch Chowder

This soup is best cooked in small batches so the conch is always tender. The bright and spicy flavors of the Jamaican jerk herbs along with the textures and colors of the conch and vegetables make a lovely soup to serve. It can be an appetizer or a main dish. Conch is sometimes hard to find; fresh or frozen clams work well in this recipe, too. See picture on page 68.

Time:
1 hour
Equipment:
Hand grinder

SERVES 4

1 potato, chopped, boiled, and
    drained
1/2 yellow onion, medium dice
2 ribs of celery, medium dice
1/2 red pepper, diced
3/4 green pepper, diced
1/8 cup olive oil
3/4 teaspoon chopped garlic
1-1/2 cup canned tomatoes in purée,
    chopped
3/4 cup water
1-1/2 tablespoons Caribbean or
    Jamaican jerk seasoning

1/2 cup white wine
1 cup clam juice
3/4 teaspoon Worcestershire sauce
1/2 teaspoon Tabasco sauce
1 pound fresh or frozen conch,
    rough ground, then finely
    chopped
1/8 cup olive oil (another one)
salt and pepper to taste
1/8 cup fresh Italian parsley,
    chopped
1/8 cup green onion, chopped

In the bottom of a soup pot, sauté the vegetables in 1/8 cup olive oil. Add the garlic, tomatoes, water, jerk seasoning, wine, clam juice, Worcestershire sauce and Tabasco. Allow to simmer. In a mixing bowl, use your hands to combine the conch and 1/8 cup of olive oil (the second one) and salt and pepper to taste. In a sauté pan, sauté the conch mixture for 30 seconds. Add the conch to the soup and simmer until all ingredients are hot. Serve the chowder with a garnish of chopped Italian parsley and green onion. In the picture on page 68, we use a 1-inch square of herbed crostini (p. 21) with a slice of mango and herbs on top for a garnish.

European-style Pilsner
No, not that flavorless, mass-marketed fizz. We're talking about a nice European style, bursting with floral hop bitterness to stand up to the spice and let the flavors sing. The beer refreshes so much between bites, it's like every bite is the first.
Blue Paddle Pilsner – New Belgium Brewing, Colorado
Pilsner Urquell – Pilsner Urquell, SAB Miller, Czech Bohemia

Shrimp Essence

Ever wonder what to do with all those shrimp shells and parsley stems? Better yet, ever wonder why anyone saves them? Well, here is an answer: extra flavor. James Davis will squeeze the last bit of flavor out of anything, including shrimp shells, to add that little extra something. This essence is the base of soups, sauces, and, for the purposes of this book, shrimp creole (p. 47-48). It has a light, peppery flavor and fragrance. Adding shrimp essence to a sauce is definitely better than adding just water. Shrimp essence will store in the freezer for three months. Wait 'til you get to the creole!

Time:
1-1/2 hours,
1 hour active

Makes 6 cups

2 tablespoons light vegetable oil
3/4 pound shrimp shells
1 tablespoon kosher salt
1 tablespoon tomato paste
1 stalk of celery, rough chopped
3 parsley stems, rough chopped
1 yellow onion, rough chopped
1 carrot, peeled and rough chopped
4 whole garlic cloves

4 sprigs of fresh thyme
1 bay leaf
2 teaspoons crushed red pepper
1 teaspoon black peppercorns
1/4 cup sherry
1/2 gallon cold water,
     approximately
salt to taste

Chef's note: Lighter oils such as canola or peanut oil get hotter than olive oil before they smoke, allowing for a more intense sautéing effect.

In a heavy-bottomed saucepan, heat oil until smoking hot. Add shrimp shells and kosher salt; stir quite often. The shells will turn bright, salmon pink.

When all the shells are bright pink, add tomato paste, the vegetables, garlic, thyme, bay leaf, crushed red peppers, and peppercorns. Cook until the onions are translucent. Add sherry and deglaze the bottom of the pan. Add water to cover the shells. Boil for 30 minutes, strain through a strainer or chinois, and then cool.

Chicken Stock

Time: 5 hours, 20 minutes active

Makes 3 quarts

Homemade chicken stock is the base for Swiss Onion Soup (p. 26) and Chicken Lime Tortilla Soup (p. 28). Whenever you have roast chicken, freeze the bones. After four or five dinners, you'll have enough to make stock. (However, guests looking for ice cubes in your freezer may wonder why you have chicken bones in there.) The stock will store for three months in the freezer.

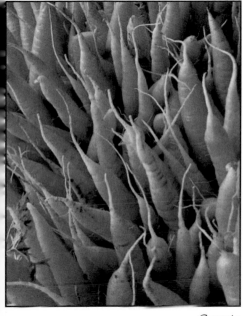

Carrots

3/4 cup onion, diced
1/2 cup celery, diced
1/8 cup carrots, diced
1 gallon cold water
1 to 1-1/2 pounds cleaned chicken bones

3 sprigs fresh thyme
10 sprigs fresh Italian parsley
2 tablespoons peppercorns
2 bay leaves

In a soup pot, combine all the ingredients and fill the pot with cold water, enough to cover the chicken bones with 3-4 inches of water. Bring the pot to a near boil and then simmer to reduce by 1/4, about 5 hours. Make sure the bones are covered with water at all times. Strain the stock and you're ready for the next step, be it a sauce or a soup.

Chef's note: To keep the stock clear, use cold water and never allow it to fully boil. Also, stocks should not be salted until they are strained and ready to be used in a soup or sauce.

Vegetable Stock

This stock is the base for Butternut Bisque (p. 27), and you can use it for Carrot Cumin Soup (p. 30) instead of mushroom stock. We encourage you to save vegetable ends and skins just for the purpose of making stock; what a great way to add flavor and color to soups while reducing waste.

Time:
1 hour,
15 minutes active

Makes 1 quart

3/4 cup carrot, chopped
3/4 cup yellow onion, chopped
3/4 cup leeks, chopped
3/4 cup celery, chopped
1 potato with skin on, 1" inch cubes
2 cloves garlic, whole
1/2 organic lemon

1 juniper berry
1 coriander seed, crushed
1 bunch of parsley
1 sprig thyme
1 sprig rosemary
2-3 peppercorns
6 cups water, approximately
1/4 cup white wine

Leek Leaves

Chef's note: If you would like more color in your stock, grill or sear the onion before you chop it.

Rinse all the vegetables very well and chop. Put all dry ingredients in a large stock pot. Put enough water in the pot to cover the vegetables, lemon, and herbs with 3 inches of water. Add wine. Simmer for 45 minutes so that the stock reduces by one-fifth. Strain.

★★★ Veal Stock, Demi-glace, Glace de Viande

Time:
8-9 hours,
2-1/2 hours
active

Makes 3 quarts stock

The difference between "very good" and "great" in a meal often starts at the base. Veal stock serves as the base for Laughing Lab Beef Chili (p. 56) and for creating the demi-glace for Gorgonzola Beef Tips (p. 59). To be sure, you can buy veal stock and demi-glace but, as James says, "It won't have your love in it." Here is how you can make the good stuff at home.

2 pounds veal bones, dry
1 gallon cold water, approximately
1 cup yellow onion, chopped
1/2 cup celery, chopped
1/2 cup carrot, chopped
1/4 cup tomato paste

1-1/2 cup red wine, any kind will do
1 teaspoon black peppercorns
12 parsley stems, chopped
2 bay leaves
2 sprigs thyme

Roast the dry veal bones in a 350° oven until they are a nice brown, rolling them every 30 minutes or so for a total of approximately 2-1/2 hours. Put roasted bones in a soup pot and add enough cold water to cover the bones by 4-6" of water. Bring pot to a boil.

While waiting for the boil, prepare the vegetables. In sauté pan, use 2 tablespoons of oil from the roasting pan to sweat the onion, celery and carrots over a medium heat. When the onions are brown and caramelized, about 20 minutes, add the tomato paste and stir to coat the vegetables.

Turn up the heat a bit on the sauté pan and add the red wine, one-third at a time. Add the peppercorns, parsley, and bay leaves. Scrape the bottom of the pan to get the fond, the good stuff stuck to the bottom of the pan. This will make a dark, burgundy brown paste. Turn down the heat and scrape the pan one more time.

Back to the soup pot, reduce the heat. Skim off the impurities that have come to the surface in the soup pot (this skimming is called dépouillage). Add the vegetable and wine mixture to the soup pot and simmer for 5-6 hours, skimming the top from time to time. When the liquid is reduced by 1/3, strain the stock through a fine sieve or cheesecloth. Now you have veal stock which can be stored in the refrigerator for a week or the freezer for six months.

Demi-glace

3 quarts of veal stock

Over a medium heat, reduce the veal stock by 1/2. You can store it in the refrigerator or freezer for six months.

Time:
2 hours
Makes 1-1/2 quarts

Glace de Viande

3 quarts of veal stock

Time:
4 hours
Makes 1-1/3 cups

Reduce the veal stock by 90 percent. Pour the very thick results into ice cube trays and allow to cool and set up. When set, wrap each cube individually. This will store in the freezer for 6 months.

Chef's commentary: What is the difference between a sauce and a gravy?

A sauce is refined. Making a sauce is a slow process of extracting the flavor from whatever you are reducing. For example, the veal demi-glace has the intensified and velvety flavors of veal. It makes a terrific base for sauces, such as the one in Gorgonzola Beef Tips (p. 59).

A gravy is quick to make. It is made from the pan drippings and fond stuck to the bottom of a pan. Add flour to the pan, deglaze it with stock or wine. Then stir in water and cook until you like the texture. You get the flavor from the pan right then and there.

Mushroom Stock

Mushroom stock is very simple to make and provides great flavor for soups and gravies. We use in it the Carrot Cumin Soup recipe (p. 30).

Time:
45 minutes

Makes 2 cups

1/2 cup yellow onion, chopped
1/2 cup of celery, chopped
1/2 cup carrot, chopped
1 tablespoon canola or vegetable oil

1/2 pound chopped mushrooms
(the ones you would normally throw away would be perfect)
3 cups water

In the bottom of the pot, sweat the onion, celery, and carrot in oil. Cook until onions are translucent. Add water and mushrooms, bring to a boil, and then reduce heat to a simmer. Reduce by one-third, about 20 minutes. Strain the bits of vegetables out of the stock. That's it.

Sun Dried Tomato Pesto

This cheesy, full-flavored pesto goes well with pasta and salads. We include it here to go with the Company Salad (p. 15) and Mojo Marinated Chicken Quesadillas (p. 10), but we feel confident that you will find many more uses for it. Heck, this stuff is great when spread on Herbed Crostini (p. 21) as an appetizer.

1 ounce (weight) or 1/4 cup of fresh, whole basil leaves
1/4 pound reggiano parmigiano cheese, grated
1 tablespoon garlic, chopped
1 teaspoon pine nuts
1 tablespoon walnut pieces

1/2 cup sun dried tomatoes packed in oil, well drained
1/2 teaspoon salt, to taste
2 teaspoons black pepper
1/2 cup olive oil
(including any of the oil drained off of the tomatoes)

Time:
25 minutes
Makes 2 cups

Combine all ingredients except the oil in a food processor or blender. Slowly add the oil while blending at a medium speed for 5 minutes. The final product is very spreadable.

Chipotle Aioli

Time:
20 minutes
Equipment:
balloon whisk

Makes 1-1/4
cups

We use this aioli as a sauce for crab cakes, but don't be limited by what we do. It could be a salad dressing; it has a lot in common with a Caesar salad dressing and the Institutional Salad Dressing (p. 14). It is also pretty good on a turkey sandwich. The additional ingredients give this sauce, some heat and tang that accent mild flavors. If you are making this recipe for the crab cakes only (p. 49), consider cutting it in half.

1 tablespoon Dijon mustard

2 egg yolks

1 cup olive oil

1 tablespoon garlic, chopped

1 shallot, finely diced

1 tablespoon parsley, chopped

1 tablespoon chipotle pepper purée*

2 tablespoons scallions, minced

2 teaspoons Worcestershire sauce

1 tablespoon lemon juice

salt and pepper to taste

Combine mustard and egg yolks. Very, very slowly add in olive oil while hand whipping or while using a blender with a wire whip attachment. Whip until the mixture is emulsified and looks like a heavy duty mayonnaise. Add garlic, shallots, parsley, chipotle pepper purée, scallions, Worcestershire sauce and lemon juice. Add salt and pepper to taste.

*You can use chipotle purée or a chipotle hot sauce that has very few ingredients.

Bomb Sauce

This dark and flavorful sauce is called bomb sauce for two good reasons. First, it is "the bomb" – a great marinade for vegetables and grilled meats and a fantastic finishing sauce for just about anything. Second, it ignites a bit when you put it on the grill, like little bombs going off. This recipe makes a lot of sauce, so decide how much you need and change the recipe accordingly.

Time:
20 minutes
Makes 1
quart

1/4 cup mushroom soy sauce

10 cloves garlic, rough chopped

2 shallots, rough chopped

1 cup balsamic vinegar

1 tablespoon black pepper

3 cups pure olive oil

1 teaspoon salt (to taste)

Combine all of the ingredients except for the olive oil in a blender and blend. Slowly add the oil as you mix until the sauce is emulsified. Add salt and pepper to taste. Refrigerate.

James Davis's Hollandaise Sauce

James Davis's hollandaise looks like the original but has a slightly bigger flavor. The mustard, Tabasco, and Worcestershire sauce add some zip and expand the number of dishes this hollandaise can accompany. We serve it with Stuffed Prince Edward Island Mussels (p. 3), and we recommend it to go with crab cakes (p. 49), any other seafood, and poached eggs, of course.

Time: 30 minutes
Equipment:
Double boiler

Makes 1-1/2 cups

2 egg yolks
1/8 cup white wine
4 ounces melted, clarified butter
    at room temperature
2 tablespoons green onion,
    sliced in circles

1 tablespoon whole grain Dijon or
    Creole mustard
1 dash Tabasco
3 pinches of salt
2 teaspoons lemon juice
1 teaspoon Worcestershire sauce

You can make this sauce in a small, metal mixing bowl over a gas burner or in the top of a double boiler – it just depends on what you have in the kitchen and what you are comfortable with. The big challenge is to temper the egg yolks but not cook them.

Balloon whisk the egg yolks and wine over low heat. Keep whisking until the drippings off the whisk almost sit on top of the mixture, forming ribbons. The mixture should increase in volume two or three times. Remove from heat and slowly drizzle in the clarified butter and whip until well blended. Add green onion, mustard, Tabasco, salt, lemon juice, and Worcestershire sauce. Blend until smooth.

Chef's notes: If the sauce seems really thick, add a few drops of room temperature water and whisk to thin. Also, you can cut this recipe in half to make half a batch (3/4 cup), but you cannot effectively make it any smaller than that.

Persillade

This bread crumb topping is used in the Crabmeat Stuffed Portobello Mushrooms (p. 50) and Stuffed Prince Edward Island Mussels (p. 3) recipes. The wine in the recipe adds flavor and allows the topping to get a little crunchy without burning. Persillade is a handy ingredient to have around; it can easily spiff up steamed vegetables and casseroles.

Time:
10 minutes
Makes
1-1/4 cups

1/8 cup olive oil
1 cup plain bread crumbs
1/8 cup white wine
1 garlic clove, finely chopped
1 shallot, finely diced

2 teaspoons fresh parsley, finely
    chopped
1/4 teaspoon thyme, fresh or dried
salt and pepper to taste

Combine the ingredients in a bowl. Stir until well mixed. You can store extra persillade in the refrigerator for up to two weeks.

Warlock Onions

Bristol Brewing Company's Winter Warlock Oatmeal Stout guarantees that these are no ordinary caramelized onions. They won't ward off or attract the dark side, but their nutty flavor makes a great topping for a Stuffed Beef Tenderloin Fillet (p. 57) and for burgers.

Time:
20 minutes

Makes
1-1/2 cups

2 medium yellow onions,
    julienne slices
1/4 cup oil, any kind will do

1/2 cup Winter Warlock
    Oatmeal Stout
1 teaspoon fresh ground black pepper

Over a medium heat, cook the onions in oil for 10 minutes. You are drawing the sugar out of the onions, so do not sauté them. Stir occasionally. When the onions are lightly browned, reduce the heat and add salt and stir. Add the stout. Cook over a low heat until the beer has evaporated, 3-4 minutes. Serve as a topping for burgers or steaks.

Chef's note: Beer tends to lend a bitter flavor if boiled at a high heat.

Entrees

Almond Rosemary Crusted Salmon

Parmesan Halibut with Red Grapes

Tito Puente Tilapia Tacos

Poached Ahi Sashimi with Cucumber Salad

Jimmy's Shrimp Creole

Louisiana Crab Cakes

Crab Stuffed Portobello Mushrooms

Grilled Quail with Tuscan White Beans

Thai Duck with Sugar Snap Peas

Grilled Lamb with Pine Nut Compound Butter

Laughing Lab Beef Chili

Stuffed Beef Tenderloin Fillet

Steak au Poivre

Portobello Gorgonzola Beef Tips

Wild Mushroom Loops with Asparagus and Red Burgundy Gastrique (vegetarian)

Just Warm Greek Pasta (vegetarian)

Moussaka Deconstructa (vegetarian)

Almond Rosemary Crusted Salmon

A Blue Star favorite, the crust gives this dish a great texture and added flavor that enhances, but doesn't hide, the salmon. The quick preparation and spare list of ingredients might make this recipe a standard in your repertoire. This preparation of fish was inspired by Certified Executive Chef Timothy Creehan of Destin, Florida. See page 68 for a photo.

Time:
25 minutes

4 5-ounce skinned fillets of salmon, about 3/4" thick
1/3 cup sliced almonds
    (be sure they are very thin)
1 teaspoon salt
1 teaspoon white pepper
1 teaspoon sweet paprika

1-1/2 teaspoons of fresh, finely chopped rosemary or 4 teaspoons ground dried rosemary
1/3 cup of flour
3/4 cup light olive oil for sauté

SERVES 4

Sauce
6 tablespoons Worcestershire sauce
3 tablespoons honey

Chef's note: If you prefer, you can have the salmon skinned at the seafood market or grocery store.

Combine the dry ingredients, crushing the almonds a bit as you do. Place the dry ingredients on a plate.

Combine Worcestershire sauce and honey in a small saucepan and reduce by one-half while you cook the fish. Set aside.

Sprinkle the salmon fillets with water and then place them, one at a time, on the dry ingredients. Press them down into the crust, turn, and press again. This will coat the fish.

Heat olive oil in sauté pan over medium-high heat to pan fry the salmon. We pan fry because of the heavy crust or breading. This requires a little more oil than a sauté would, but the results are crispier. Pan fry 30 seconds and then flip. Turn down heat, continue to cook until desired doneness. At the Blue Star we serve our salmon pink in the middle which takes 2-3 minutes.

Place fillets on plate and drizzle with Worcestershire and honey sauce. Serve with saffron rice (p.77) and steamed or stir-fried vegetables.

Although this is fish, try a lighter red with salmon.
**Vavasour Pinot Noir "Dashwood" from New Zealand
Rodano Chianti Classico Riserva from Italy**

Parmesan Crusted Halibut
with Red Grapes

Time:
30 minutes

When halibut is in season, May and June, try this. The dense halibut steak is offset by the crispy cheese and sweet, juicy grapes in the topping. This can be prepared in advance and popped in the oven to bake 10 minutes before you are ready to serve.

SERVES 4

Topping
1 cup sliced red grapes
4 tablespoons Italian parsley,
    chopped
3 teaspoons olive oil
4 teaspoons shallots, thinly sliced
    and then rough chopped
3 teaspoons white balsamic vinegar
2 pinches of black pepper

1 pinch of salt

Halibut
4 halibut steaks or halibut fillets,
    6-7 ounces each
4 teaspoons mayonnaise
salt and pepper to taste
8 tablespoons shredded parmesan
1/4 cup olive oil

Preheat oven to 350°. Combine ingredients for the topping and reserve. Oil a baking sheet with olive oil. Place the steaks on the baking sheet. Rub the top of each halibut steak with 1 teaspoon of mayonnaise. Salt and pepper to taste. Sprinkle 2 tablespoons of shredded parmesan on each steak. Bake for 10 minutes – but watch it because it cooks fast. To brown the cheese, pop the steaks under a broiler for 2 minutes. Evenly divide the grape topping over the steaks. Serve with saffron rice (p. 77) and steamed veggies.

Chef's note: I really love the taste and appearance of champagne grapes with this dish. If you can put your hands on some, use whole, champagne grapes instead of sliced, red grapes.

A white to go along with the halibut, rich to go along with the parmesan
Jewel Viognier, California
Landmark Chardonnay "Overlook"

Tito Puente Tilapia Tacos

Why bring one of the finest salsa musicians of our time into the kitchen? What connection is there between Tito and tacos? Good questions. We thank former Executive Chef Dan Bailey for creating and naming this dish. This meal is assembled in a several stages and relies on other recipes in this book. Each has its role in the overall effect of this belly-warming, taste-bud-tickling plate of really good food. See picture on page 68.

Time:
30 minutes if you have all the ingredients on hand. Add an 1-1/2 to make Fruity Guacamole, Pico de Gallo, Green Rice, and Regina's Black Beans (if you soaked the beans already)

3 cups **Fruity Guacamole** (p. 78)
3 cups **Regina's Black Beans** (p. 79)
1 cup **Pico de Gallo** (p. 80)
4 **tilapia fillets**, 6-8 ounces
    (**swordfish** works well, too)
oil to cover the bottom of the
    sauté pan

salt and pepper to taste
16 **corn tortillas**
1 cup **shaved green cabbage**
2 cups **Green Rice** (p. 77)

SERVES 4

Heat the oil in a sauté pan. Sprinkle the fish with salt and pepper and sauté it, 2 minutes a side. Take fish out of the pan, cut each piece in half, and keep warm.

Prepare the corn tortillas by lightly steaming them or lightly toasting them in oil. The idea is to make the tortillas pliable.

For each serving, place a double layer of tortillas on a plate, place the cooked tilapia on top and fold the tortillas over the fish. Serve quickly because the tortillas will harden. Surround the taco with shaved cabbage, Regina's Black Beans, Fruity Guacamole, Green Rice, and Pico de Gallo. You can also serve with sour cream, chopped jalapeños, and lime wedges. Make it pretty! Serves 4.

Chef's note: Using a double layer of corn tortillas makes the tacos more durable for the diners who handle them.

Belgian-style Wheat Beer (Witbier)
This beer is an attractive, hazy style spiced with coriander and orange peel. Its bright, fresh character, along with its citrus and spice notes, match beautifully with the fish, pico, and cabbage.
Allagash White -- Allagash Brewing, Maine
Hoegaarden White -- Hoegaarden, Belgium

Poached Ahi Sashimi
with Cucumber Salad

Time:
3 hours

Equipment:
Coffee filter or
Cheese cloth
Wok
Very, very sharp knife
Cooking thermometer

We thank Tak Kim for updating this Japanese dish while using traditional complements: cucumber salad, rice, and condiments. If you decide to make it all from scratch, preparation for this dinner can take all afternoon, so get some nice green or jasmine tea to enjoy while you cook. Your guests will marvel at the delicately flavored, tender ahi, and the bright-flavored and colorful salad. See a picture of this entrée on page 69.

SERVES 4

Ahi
1-1/2 pounds of sushi grade ahi
3/4 cup kosher salt

Flavored Oil
5 cups light oil (soy, canola, sunflower)
1 cup fresh mint or cilantro
    (depends on the flavor you want
    to give the ahi)

Cucumber Salad
2 cucumbers, peeled, seeded, and
    julienned
1 small red bell pepper, julienned
1 small red onion, julienned

1 teaspoon garlic, minced
1 teaspoon crushed red pepper flakes
1/2 cup su (Japanese sweet vinegar)
1/8 cup granulated sugar
1/4 cup mirin or sake
a pinch of salt

2 cups sticky rice, prepared (p. 77)

Condiments
4 teaspoons wasabi
4 teaspoons pickled ginger
4 ounces soy sauce

Chef's note: You can purchase herb-flavored oil, if you do not want to make it.

Several of the steps in this recipe require time to rest, so the stages overlap. Start by crusting the ahi with kosher salt and letting it sit in the refrigerator for 2 or 3 hours.

If you decide to make your own flavored oil, combine oil and herb and cook in a large sauce pot at 180° for 30 minutes. It is important that the oil does not get too hot. (If the oil turns dark, you have lost the flavor.) Remove from heat and steep the oil for 1 hour. Strain the herbs out of the oil with a coffee filter or cheese cloth.

While the oil is steeping, make the cucumber salad. Combine the cucumbers, red bell pepper, onion, garlic, and pepper flakes with 1/4 cup of su (you'll use the other 1/4 cup when you plate it). In a sauce pan, combine sugar, mirin or sake, and salt. Heat the mixture until the sugar melts. As soon as the liquid is clear, it is done. Do not boil. Combine vegetables with the sauce and refrigerate for 1 hour.

Prepare sticky rice (p. 77).

When the ahi, oil, cucumber salad, and rice are ready, cook the ahi. Brush off the salt crust with as little water as possible. Heat the flavored oil in the wok to 250°. Immediately put the ahi in the oil and poach for 1 minute for rare, 2 minutes for medium rare. Slice the fish against the grain into 3/8" thick slices. Use a very sharp knife or the fish will crumble.

To plate this entrée, place a mound of rice in the middle of each plate and drizzle with one-quarter of the remaining su. For each plate, place one-quarter of the cucumber salad on one side of the rice and on the other, place one-quarter of the ahi. Garnish the ahi with springs of the fresh herb used in oil. Serve with 1 tablespoon of wasabi, 1 teaspoon of pickled ginger, and a small dish of soy sauce.

Close up of Poached Ahi Sashimi

MAN Vintners Chenin Blanc from South Africa
Nigl Gruner Veltliner from Austria

Jimmy's Shrimp Creole

Time: 1 hour, if you
have shrimp essence
on hand.
Add 1-1/2 hours to
make shrimp essence

Equipment: skewers

SERVES 4

Shrimp creole, by its very nature, is a product of many influences. The many layers of flavor in this creole may surprise you. Make it according to the recipe the first time and then use it as a backdrop for your own ideas. It is easy to overwhelm the mélange of flavors in this dish with the heat of the peppers and Tabasco, so taste it as you go along. You can always make it hotter if you want, but you can't go the other way. You won't be lonely in the kitchen while you make this dish; the fragrance will start bringing people in to see what is going on.

2-1/2 cups yellow onions, medium chopped
2-1/2 cups celery, medium chopped
2 cups green bell peppers, chopped
1/2 cup red bell peppers, chopped
1/2 pound butter
1-1/2 tablespoons chopped garlic
1-1/2 teaspoons fresh thyme
1 tablespoon fresh basil, chopped
2 bay leaves
1/2 cup white wine
1/2 teaspoon cayenne
1 tablespoon black pepper
3/4 teaspoon white pepper

2 cups shrimp essence (p. 32)
1/4 cup Worcestershire sauce
1 tablespoon Tabasco
4 cups canned, chopped tomatoes, with liquid
1 cup chopped green onions
1/2 cup fresh Italian parsley, chopped

2 tablespoons cornstarch
2 tablespoons water

1-1/4 pound shrimp, shelled and deveined
2 tablespoons olive oil
salt and pepper to taste

We start with the holy trinity of Cajun cooking: onion, celery, and bell peppers. Sauté them in the butter (yes, all the butter) until onions are translucent. Add the garlic, thyme, basil, and bay leaves; let the vegetables cook until they are all soft. Add the wine, cayenne, black pepper, and white pepper. Simmer for 5 minutes.

Fresh Shrimp

Add the shrimp essence and stir. Add the Worcestershire sauce, Tabasco, and tomatoes. Stir it up well and add the chopped green onion and parsley. Taste the creole and adjust the flavor by adding pepper or Tabasco. Bring to a boil.

In a separate bowl, combine the water and cornstarch to make a slurry. When the creole is boiling, add the slurry and stir until desired thickness. Turn down the heat and let simmer until you are ready to serve.

While the creole is simmering, grill the shrimp by placing them on skewers, rub with olive oil and salt and pepper to taste. Grill until the shrimp are opaque – the time will depend on the heat of your grill. You can also sauté the shrimp in butter on the stove. Again, cook until opaque.

To show off the shrimp, serve with creole on the bottom, rice on the creole, and top with cooked shrimp. Garnish with scallions. Serves 4 with leftovers, and you will want these leftovers.

Chef's note: Once you have the creole, you can use any kind of fish or meat that you want on top of it. Grilled andouille sausages are great. Mix it up and see what happens. If you use shrimp as suggested, freeze those shells for the next batch of shrimp essence.

American-style Pale Ale or IPA
These styles showcase the almighty hop with a citrus, floral, earthy bitterness that grabs the robust flavors of this dish. The flavor and aroma of the citrus character in particular will dance with the spice.
Wet Mountain IPA – Il Vicino Brewing, New Mexico & **Colorado**
Liberty Ale – Anchor Brewing, California

Louisiana Crab Cakes

This recipe uses very little binding, so the taste of the crab meat stands out. We recommend that you splurge with lump or claw crab meat. These meaty cakes are full of tastes, textures, and have a little zip. Use the recipe as the foundation for your crab cake experiments; for example, add other flavors with a tablespoon of Worcestershire sauce, chopped onions, celery, or fresh red bell pepper.

Time:
40 minutes,
if you have
Chipotle Aioli
on hand
Add 20 minutes
to make the aioli

SERVES 4

1 pound canned, pasteurized, or frozen cooked blue crab meat (lump or claw)
1/4 cup mayonnaise
2 tablespoons coarse grain Dijon mustard
1/4 teaspoon curry
1/2 teaspoon fresh chopped garlic
1/4 cup green onion greens, finely chopped
1/4 cup grated pecorino romano cheese

salt and black pepper to taste
a pinch of cayenne
1 teaspoon lemon juice
1 egg, beaten
2 teaspoons Marsala wine
6 tablespoons bread crumbs, plus 3 tablespoons for coating
1/4 cup olive oil
1/2 cup Chipotle Aioli (p. 38)

Preheat oven to 350°. Mix together crab meat, mayonnaise, mustard, curry, garlic, green onion, romano, salt, pepper, cayenne, lemon juice, egg and marsala. Gently stir so as not to break up the crab meat. [If you are making the crab mixture for Crab Stuffed Portobello Mushrooms (p. 50), stop here.]

Form 8 crab cakes approximately the size of the palm of your hand and 1 inch thick. Because there is little binding in the mixture, be sure to press the cakes firmly so they stay together during the cooking. Gently coat the cakes with 3 tablespoons bread crumbs. Heat olive oil in sauté pan. Sauté the cakes on each side until brown, about 2 minutes. Turn crab cakes delicately and watch out for the moisture of the crab popping onto your skin while sautéing. Place in oven, in the sauté pan or on an oven-proof dish, and bake for 5 minutes at 350°. Serves 4 with two crab cakes per person. Serve with 1 tablespoon of Chipotle Aioli per crab cake, Saffron Rice (p. 77), and vegetables of your choice.

Chef's notes: You can also serve these with James Davis's Hollandaise (p. 39). Consider grating a lot of pecorino romano just to have it around to add to dishes. You can keep it in your refrigerator or freezer.

A rich white to match the rich crab.
Cartlidge and Brown Chardonnay from California
Newton, Unfiltered Chardonnay from Napa

Crab Stuffed Portobello Mushrooms

A rich, flavorful, and textured lunch or dinner entrée. Use our Louisiana Crab Cake recipe for the stuffing and the persillade recipe for a topping. This appears more complicated than it is and will make you look great in front of your family or guests.

Time: 55 minutes, including making the crab stuffing and persillade

SERVES 4

1 cup Louisiana Crab Cake mix (p. 49)
4 portobello mushroom caps
1/2 cup persillade (p. 40)

Portobello Mushrooms

Preheat oven to 350°.
Lightly brush the mushroom caps with a cloth to remove any dirt. Place on a hot grill, smooth side down, and grill until they start to sweat a bit. Remove from grill.

Fill each cap with crab mixture and top with persillade. Place on a baking pan and heat in the oven until the persillade turns golden brown and the crab is warm, about 7-10 minutes. Serve with Saffron Rice (p. 77) or simple mixed greens.

To complement the mushroom (there is more of it than crab), but still on the lighter side.
Bruno Clair Rosé from Marsannay, France
Bethel Heights Pinot Noir from Willamette Valley, Oregon

Grilled Quail
with Tuscan White Beans

Time:
30 minutes

The quail provides a strong flavor that accents the Tuscan white beans, which tend to steal the show. The strong flavors of garlic and basil are highlighted by balsamic vinegar. The beans are made creamy and flavorful by pecorino romano, parmesan cheese, and oil. You can make the beans in advance, which leaves you free to mingle with your guests until you grill the quail.

Tuscan White Beans

3 cups Great Northern beans, cooked

1/2 small red onion, minced

1/3 cup basil, finely chopped

1/3 cup grated pecorino romano cheese

1/3 cup grated parmesan cheese

1/2 cup olive oil

1/4 cup dark balsamic vinegar

1 teaspoon of fresh ground black pepper

1 teaspoon of minced garlic

salt and pepper to taste

Combine ingredients and refrigerate before serving.

Chef's notes: If you don't like the brownish color dark balsamic vinegar gives the beans, you can use white balsamic vinegar. I think the dark tastes better, though. Also, be aware that the cheese is salty, so you may need very little extra salt.

Grilled Quail

8 quail, semi-boneless (with leg bone only)
1/2 cup olive oil
salt and pepper to taste

Time:
20 minutes,
once the grill
is hot

Italian Parsley

SERVES
4

Rub the quail with oil and sprinkle with salt and pepper to taste. Grill quail for 2-3 minutes a side. Place two quail on each of 4 dishes and serve with Tuscan White Beans and some sort of greens, such as fresh or wilted kale, spinach or escarole. Garnish with Italian parsley.

How can you not serve an Italian wine with those Tuscan White Beans?

For a lighter-style red, **Villa Guilia Chianti "Alaura"** will be perfect. The wine itself is a good story, too. The wine was created by a wine-making couple to serve at their wedding, and the painting of horses on the label is what they received as a wedding gift.

Staying with lighter red, but more complex, **La Massa Giorgio Primo**. Another great story: The winemaker raced motorcycles for a living, then decided to slow down, make wine. After being refused by his parents when he asked for funding, he asked his uncle Giorgio, who agreed. In gratitude, he named the wine after him, and it is now one of the greatest wines to come out of Tuscany.

Thai Duck
with Sugar Snap Peas

This is easier than you might think, and it looks and tastes terrific. The rich flavor and texture of duck is set off by the hot and sweet Thai sauce. The sugar snap peas add color and crunch to make this entrée a lot of fun to eat. See picture on page 71.

Time:
30 Minutes

SERVES 4

4 duck breasts
1/4 cup kosher salt
4 cups fresh sugar snap peas, strings removed
2 tablespoons of peanut oil or duck fat from cooking the breasts
salt and white pepper to taste

1/2 teaspoons salad oil
2 cups sticky rice (p. 77)
8 oz. sweet Thai chili sauce (we like Mae Ploy brand sauce)

Score the skin of the duck breast in a cross hatch, then liberally salt. Place duck, skin side down, in dry, hot sauté pan for 1 minute. Reduce heat to medium until the duck skin gets brown and crispy, about 3 minutes. Flip the breasts over and cook for 3 minutes. Flip again and cook for another 3 minutes.

Remove from heat and let rest for 5 minutes. Slice each breast into 1/8 " thick, bias slices. The meat will be done to medium to medium rare. Strain the duck fat from pan and reserve; it is great to cook with (see Regina's Black Beans p. 79).

Sauté peas in 2 tablespoons of the duck fat or use peanut oil. Add salt and white pepper to taste.

Press 1/2 cup of sticky rice into a lightly oiled cup or small bowl to mold the rice. In the middle of the plate, invert the cup and gently knock out the rice. Place the slices of one duck breast in a fan on one side of the mound of rice and place 1/4 of the sugar snap peas on the other side. Drizzle duck with sweet Thai chili sauce, 2 ounces a serving. Garnish with fresh cilantro sprigs or daikon sprouts. You could also sprinkle with black sesame seeds.

Ah, the lovely duck with a great pinot noir!
David Bruce, Central Coast
Any pinot noir from Archery Summit

Grilled Lamb Loin
with Pine Nut Compound Butter

This magical entrée makes its own sauce on top as you serve it. The compound butter melts in place and stays on the meat so that all the flavors can combine in every single bite. Nothing about this dish is difficult, but you will need to prepare the compound butter a day in advance so that it freezes solid. See a picture on page 69.

Time:
30 minutes,
then overnight
in the freezer
Equipment:
parchment
paper

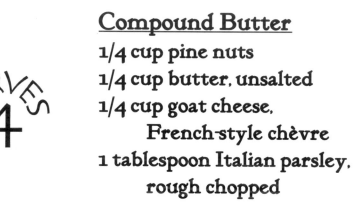

SERVES 4

Compound Butter

1/4 cup pine nuts

1/4 cup butter, unsalted

1/4 cup goat cheese,
    French-style chèvre

1 tablespoon Italian parsley,
    rough chopped

a pinch of salt and pepper,
    to taste

2 teaspoons shallots, diced

1/2 teaspoon Worcestershire
    sauce

1/4 teaspoon lemon juice

1/2 teaspoon minced garlic

Roast pine nuts on a baking sheet for 5-6 minutes in a 300° oven and cool.

Whip the butter and goat cheese at a high speed for 10 minutes. This step whips air into the butter and cheese to make them lighter and the flavors more delicate. At a slow speed, add in parsley, salt, and pepper. Then add shallots, Worcestershire sauce, lemon juice, and garlic. Blend thoroughly. By hand, mix in the whole roasted pine nuts. The final mixture will be a bit sloppy.

Now you are going to use the parchment paper to make a 6" long roll out of the mixture that is 1-1/2" in diameter. The trick for making a roll even is to place the mixture lengthwise in a crease in the middle of a piece of parchment paper. With the upper layer of parchment covering the roll, use the edge of a cookie sheet to push against the parchment at the bottom, lengthwise edge of the roll. This will wrap the parchment tightly around the butter roll. Roll it over one time to keep the shape. The roll will be flimsy, so place it on a cookie sheet in the freezer at least overnight.

Grilled Lamb Loin

Time: 30 minutes.

1-1/2 to 1-3/4 pounds whole lamb loins,
allowing 6-7 oz. per person
1/4 cup olive oil
2 tablespoons lemon juice
1 tablespoon white vinegar
2 tablespoons kosher salt
2 tablespoons cracked black pepper

Close up of Compount Butter Melting on a Lamb Loin

Chef's note: Lamb loins can be hard to find, so you can use lamb chops or racks of lamb, too. Allow 3 nice-sized chops or 4 ribs from the rack per person.

Prehcat the grill. Combine olive oil, lemon juice, and vinegar. Coat the lamb loins with olive oil mixture. Combine salt and pepper on a plate and roll the lamb in it to lightly coat. Sear the meat on the grill and then reduce the heat to cook it to the doneness of your liking. Times will vary depending on how hot your grill is.

Divide the loins over four plates. Put two or three one-quarter inch thick slices of pine nut compound butter on each piece of meat. This is the good stuff! Serve with Blue Star House Mashers (p. 76) and steamed or blanched vegetables.

Chef's note: If you have leftover compound butter, you can use it to stuff chicken breasts for the grill or oven. Save a little to put on top, too. It is also good on crackers or crostini if it is softened.

Only a big and bold wine will be able to hold its own against the lamb and goat cheese.
Martin Ray, Cabernet Sauvignon "Angeline"
Penfolds, Cabernet Sauvignon Bin 707

Laughing Lab Beef Chili

This beef and corn chili has a rich flavor, a luscious sauce, and just enough heat. The Laughing Lab Ale guarantees you that will put a smile on your guests' faces. And to top it off, it uses only one pan.

Time: 45 minutes, if you have veal or beef stock on hand. Add 8 hours to make veal or beef stock

1/4 cup olive oil
1 pound beef cubes or ground beef
1/2 yellow onion, diced
1 tablespoon garlic, chopped
1 tablespoon cumin
2 tablespoons chili powder
2 tablespoons flour
2 cups veal or beef stock (p. 35)
1-1/2 cups tomatoes, canned

1 tablespoon honey
1 tablespoon Worcestershire sauce
1-1/2 teaspoons of srirachi chile paste
2 cups corn confetti (p. 78)
1/4 cup of Laughing Lab ale
salt and pepper to taste
1/2 cup shredded cheddar cheese
1/4 cup red onion, chopped

SERVES 4

Heat the olive oil in a large frying pan. Sear the meat until it is dry* to get the most flavor for the chili. Stir in the onions, garlic, cumin, and chili powder and cook until the onions are translucent. Stir in the flour while scraping the bottom of the pan.

Add the stock, tomatoes, honey, Worcestershire sauce, and srirachi paste. Stir while scraping the fond from the bottom of the pan. Simmer until a sauce forms, about 15 minutes. If you haven't already made the corn confetti, now is a good time.

Stir in the corn confetti and Laughing Lab. Do not boil once the beer is in the chili or it might get bitter. Add salt and pepper to taste.

Divide into four big bowls; serve with House Mashers (p. 76) and steamed green beans. Top with shredded cheese and red onions.

Chef's note: When you sear meat, there is a point when it looks like it is boiling. Keep cooking the meat until the boiling stops and only oil and browned meat remain. This adds flavor to the pan; it's called fond.

Laughing Lab Scottish Ale -- what else?
Scottish Ales are characterized by a round maltiness with hints of nuts, smoke, roast, and caramel. This beer draws out the caramelized sweetness of the meat and matches the earthy character of the spice beautifully.
Laughing Lab Scottish Ale -- Bristol Brewing, Colorado

Stuffed Beef Tenderloin Fillet

If you are not too worried about your cholesterol count (or you choose to ignore it for a few hours), this entrée will give you your steak fix with a treat in the middle – gorgonzola cheese, porcini mushrooms, or both. As with most cooking, the better your ingredients, the better the results. This dish is easy to prepare in advance and cooks at the last minute. You may never cook an unstuffed steak again.

Time:
30 minutes

SERVES 4

The Steaks

4 fillets of beef tenderloin,
     7 ounces each
2 tablespoons olive oil
salt and pepper to taste

Gorgonzola filling

4 ounces gorgonzola cheese

No preparation needed.

Porcini Mushroom filling

1/2 cup porcini mushrooms, rough chopped
1 shallot, minced
1 tablespoon butter
splash of red wine
salt and pepper to taste

Melt the butter in a sauté pan, add mushrooms and shallot. Cook until the shallot is transparent. Deglaze pan with wine. Add salt and pepper to taste

---

Prepare the filling(s) of your choice. Using a sharp knife, make a 1/2 inch slice in the side of the fillets and move the knife back and forth inside the fillet to make a pocket in the middle of the steak. Try to keep the opening in the side of the steak small so the stuffing stays inside while grilling.

Stuff each fillet with 1/4 of the filling, being sure to distribute it throughout the steak. Oil the outside of the fillet and lightly salt and pepper. Grill 4 minutes a side or until cooked to desired doneness. You can top with Warlock Onions (p. 40) and serve with House Mashers (p. 76).

Chef's notes:
Warning! Pay attention while you are grilling. Stuffed steaks cook faster than unstuffed ones, and it can be tricky to get an accurate temperature reading, too.

Wrapping a slice of bacon around the meat and securing it with a toothpick will impart extra flavor and will help hold the stuffing in the steak. This is called barding.

The proteins from the fillet will marry well with the tannins in dry reds.
Perrin, Cotes du Rhone Reserve
Howell Mountain, Cabernet Sauvignon

Steak au Poivre

*This classic entrée is best with top-quality ingredients.
Use well-aged beef tenderloin and heavy cream, and your
dining companions will think you are a genius.*

Time:
20 minutes
25 minutes
for well done

SERVES 4

Four fillets of beef tenderloin, 6-8 ounces
3 tablespoons black pepper, coarsely ground
6 tablespoons of oil
1 cup heavy cream
salt to taste

Cream, Peppercorns, and Tenderloin Fillet.

Preheat oven to 350°.
Place pepper on a flat dish. Press one side of the meat into the pepper, coating it with as much pepper as it will hold.

Heat the oil in a sauté pan. Sear both sides of the meat and then sear the edges. Place sauté pan, meat and all, in the pre-heated oven to cook meat a bit more. Pull the meat out of the oven when it is 10° below the desired temperature.

Make sure the pepper side is down, return the pan to the stove top, and add the cream and salt. Let the sauce bubble for 3-4 minutes. It will get brownish and thick; it should reduce to about 1/3 cup. Place the fillets on plates and pour the sauce over them. Serve with House Mashers (p. 76) and steamed vegetables.

Big and red and spicy!
Trapiche Malbec Oak Cask from Argentina
Robert Biale Zinfandel, Monte Rosso Vineyard

Portobello Gorgonzola Beef Tips

This is a rich and delicious entrée much loved by Blue Star patrons. Its velvety demi-glace and tangy blue cheese separate this dish from the ordinary beef tips. Smaller portions are a perfect luncheon while more generous servings with House Mashers (p. 76) and vegetables provide an elegant and ample dinner. We have a picture on page 70.

Time:
After you have the demi-glace, 25 minutes

Before you start:
There is a variety of ways to get demi-glace. You can make it from scratch (p. 36). You can buy it (see page 93), or you can buy canned beef broth and reduce it times 8. Once you have the demi-glace, this is a relatively simple dish to prepare. But be warned; don't skip the demi-glace — it doesn't taste as good without it.

extra virgin olive oil to cover pan

20 ounces beef tips, 2" x 2" pieces from
      New York strip or filet mignon

2 shallots, shaved

2 portobello mushrooms, sliced thin

1/4 cup red wine, a cabernet is nice

1/3 cup beef demi-glace (p. 36)

1/2 cup gorgonzola cheese, crumbled

2 tablespoons unsalted butter

SERVES 4

Heat olive oil in a hot sauté pan. Sear one side of the beef tips for 1 minute, and then turn down the heat to medium and brown the other side. Add the shallots and mushrooms, sauté for 2 minutes. Deglaze the pan with the wine and reduce the mixture for 2-3 minutes. Add the demi-glace and stir until it begins to look like a rich, brown glaze, 3-4 minutes. Add the crumbled cheese and butter, reducing it into the sauce until the cheese is melted, another minute. The glaze will lighten in color and thicken. Serve immediately with House Mashers (p. 76), steamed vegetables, and garnish with more gorgonzola crumbled on the top. Serves 4.

Chef's note: If you prefer your tips to be less done, simply remove the meat from the sauté pan before adding the shallots and mushrooms, then return the meat to the pan during the cheese and butter stage.

Earthy to match the portobellos, red to pair with the gorgonzola and beef.
Domaine Lafite Rothschild, Pauillac (a secondary label from the pricey stuff)
Steltzner Cabernet, Stags Leap District

Wild Mushroom Loops
with Asparagus and Red Burgundy Gastrique

★ ★ ★

The vegetarians in your life will be ever so happy that you learned about this one. This hearty entrée is full of earthy flavors that are set off by the bright, tart Red Burgundy Gastrique. It has lots of ingredients, lots of steps, and you have to be patient with the phyllo dough, but you will be rewarded. It is beautiful on the plate and very, very tasty. See a picture of this dish on page 70. The mushroom loops freeze well, and can be warmed and sliced for a tapa.

Time:
1 hour and
45 minutes
Equipment:
Damp towel
Pastry brush
Baking sheet
Steamer

1 cup forest mixture of dried
    mushrooms, rough chopped

1/3 cup unsalted butter to sauté in

1/2 yellow onion, julienned

2 tablespoon garlic, minced

2 fresh portobello mushroom caps,
    rough chopped

2 dozen fresh white mushroom
    caps, chopped

1 teaspoon ground black pepper

1/2 teaspoon kosher salt

2 tablespoon fresh Italian parsley,
    chopped

2 tablespoons fresh basil, chopped

4 scallion greens, 1/4 inch slices

3/4 cup butter to melt

12 sheets of phyllo dough

20 stalks of asparagus

1/2 cup Red Burgundy Gastrique(p. 61)

SERVES 4

Soak the chopped, dried mushrooms in water for 30 minutes until they are rehydrated. Drain. Preheat oven to 350°. While the mushrooms are soaking, make the gastrique.

Red Burgundy Gastrique

A gastrique is a syrupy reduction of sugar and vinegar.
The sweet tart flavor of this sauce is perfect for the Wild Mushroom Loops.

Time:
10 minutes

1/4 cup sugar
1/4 cup red wine
1/8 cup red wine vinegar

Makes 1/2 cup

Combine the sugar and red wine. Heat over a medium heat until the mixture gets frothy and syrupy, 4-5 minutes. Add vinegar and stir. Cool until syrupy again.

When the mushrooms are rehydrated, start cooking the filling for the mushroom loops. In a large, hot sauté pan, melt 1/3 cup butter. Sauté garlic and onions until translucent. Add all the mushrooms and sauté for 5 minutes. Add black pepper, kosher salt, parsley, basil, and scallion greens. Cook over a medium heat for 5 more minutes.* Turn down the heat to low to keep the pan warm.

In a small sauce pan, melt 3/4 cup of butter and place a damp towel on the countertop. Place one sheet of phyllo on the towel and brush it with melted butter. Add a second layer of phyllo and brush with butter. Add a third layer of phyllo. Put 1/4 of the mushroom mixture in a log shape on the dough, along the long edge. Fold in the short edges of the phyllo and roll up the mushroom mixture as if it were a loose egg roll, see picture on page 94. Brush with butter (again) and gently form the roll in a loop shape, and – you guessed it – brush with butter. The loops may crack a little as you shape them – that's okay, just be very gentle. Make four mushroom loops. Using a spatula, gently place the loops on a baking sheet and bake in a 350° oven until golden brown, approximately 20 minutes.

While the loops are baking, steam 20 asparagus stalks for 3 minutes. When the loops are baked, put one on each plate with five asparagus stalks tucked into the curve of the loop and drizzle with 2 tablespoons of Red Burgundy Gastrique. You can serve with Blue Star House Mashers, if you wish (p. 76).

*At this point, you could use this mixture to stuff poultry or a steak.

Chef's note: When you melt butter, it tends to separate into milk solids and fat. When brushing the phyllo with butter, try to evenly distribute both parts of the melted butter on each layer. It makes the loops more pliable in the looping stage.

Something with a bit of earthiness to it to complement the mushrooms.
Heron Merlot, Vin de Pays, France
Castellare di Castellina, I Sodi di San Niccolò from Italy

Just Warm Greek Pasta

Watch the plates empty before your very eyes. A colorful mixture of pasta and Greek goodies, this entrée has a bright taste and appearance as well as terrific textures. Extra servings store well in the refrigerator for a few days. We suggest that you serve it warm, but you can also serve it cold. Take it to the next potluck, and you will be going home with an empty serving bowl.

Time:
40 minutes

2 cups dried orzo
1/2 cup calamata olives, pitted and chopped
1/2 cup sun dried tomatoes, chiffonade
1 tablespoon fresh basil, chiffonade
6 canned pepperoncini peppers, chiffonade
1 cup fresh spinach cut in 3/8" ribbons

1/2 cup olive oil
1 tablespoon garlic, minced
4 tablespoons balsamic vinegar
      (white or dark, whichever you prefer)
salt and ground pepper to taste
4 tablespoons crumbled feta cheese

Boil 2 quarts of water and add orzo. Cook until the pasta is al dente and drain.

While the pasta is boiling, prepare the olives, sun-dried tomatoes, basil, peppers and spinach. The more carefully you prepare these ingredients, the more beautiful your results will be. Combine the olives, sun dried tomatoes, peppers, basil, and spinach in a large mixing bowl.

In a sauté pan, heat oil, and then add garlic. Toast the garlic in the oil until the oil froths a bit. Quickly pour oil and garlic over vegetables. Add the drained pasta and add the balsamic vinegar. Add salt and pepper to taste (we like to be a bit heavy with the pepper). Divide over 4 plates and crumble 1 tablespoon of feta on each plate. Serve just warm.

Greek wine with this dish, don't you think? Think crisp reds.
Domaine Skouras, St. George, from the Nemea region of Greece
Ktima Karyda, Naoussa

Moussaka Deconstructa

Instead of the usual layered casserole moussaka, this dish deconstructs the casserole and preserves the textures and flavors of each vegetable as well as adding some of the flavor from the grill. This more healthful version is fun to eat and looks lovely in presentation.

Time: 1 hour of advance preparation (a day or several hours before meal); 30 minutes at serving time
Equipment: Grill or grill pan

SERVES 4

8 roma tomatoes
1 cup extra virgin olive oil
10 cloves of garlic
1 eggplant, peeled
1/2 teaspoon salt
12 small, new potatoes with skin on
1 red pepper, quartered
1 red onion, cut in 1/4 inch slices
1 pound of fresh spinach
1/4 cup of Chablis wine

1 tablespoon olive oil
salt and pepper to taste
2 pita pockets

<u>Nutmeg-cinnamon goat cheese:</u>
(makes 4 ounces)
1/4 teaspoon grated nutmeg
1/2 teaspoon cinnamon
1/2 cup goat cheese,
　　　French-style chèvre

Prepare in advance the tomatoes, potatoes, and eggplant. You can do these at the same time to save time and olive oil. We are going to use the infused oil made for the tomatoes for everything in this recipe. Also prepare the nutmeg-cinnamon goat cheese.

Tomatoes: Place 1 cup of olive oil and 10 cloves of garlic in a pan and warm to 200°. Place whole tomatoes in oil and slowly blanch the tomatoes for 30 minutes. This is tomato confit. Carefully remove the tomatoes from the oil and refrigerate until you are ready to make the main attraction. Reserve the tomato-garlic infused oil.

Eggplant: Slice the eggplant into 1" thick rounds and salt the slices with 1/2 teaspoon of salt. In ten minutes, you'll see water beading up on the slices. The salt removes the bitterness of the eggplant. Pat the slices dry, drizzle with one-half of the tomato-garlic infused oil.

Potatoes: Boil the new potatoes, cool them. Place them in a container with the remaining infused oil. Refrigerate.

Make the nutmeg-cinnamon goat cheese by blending the nutmeg, cinnamon, and goat cheese.

30 minutes from serving.

Preheat oven to 350°. Warm the grill or grill pan.

Place the whole tomatoes and potatoes on an oven proof dish or skillet, salt and pepper lightly. Reserve the oil. Put vegetables into a 350° oven to warm, about 5 minutes.

Pepper eggplant. Salt and pepper red pepper quarters and red onion slices, and drizzle everything with some of the oil from the tomato confit.   Grill eggplant, peppers and onions over a medium heat until they have a grill mark and are warm but before they get carbon build-up, 5 minutes. Put the potatoes on the grill in the last 2 minutes to give them a grill mark, too.

Place the grilled vegetables on the same plate with the tomatoes and leave in oven until hot, 3 minutes. The combination will create its own sauce on the plate.

While the vegetables are in the oven, wilt the spinach in 1 tablespoon of hot olive oil in a sauté pan. Add a splash of Chablis.

Place equal amounts of spinach in the middle of each of four plates. Divide and arrange the vegetables in layers around and on top of the spinach. Drizzle with the drippings on the dish from the oven. Crumble 1 ounce of nutmeg-cinnamon goat cheese on the top of each serving.

Brush pita with the tomato confit oil and warm in oven.

Place the plates under a broiler or put in the top of the oven for 3 minutes to melt and brown the cheese a bit.

When the broiling phase is over, cut the pita into sixths and place the pita wedges in amongst the layers of vegetables. Serve.

Chef's note: If you choose to add more grilled veggies from the icebox, feel free. Also, one of our kitchen testers used the same idea to create deconstructed, vegetable lasagna. We are not sure how she did it, but she liked it.

Eggplant

A brightly flavored red, not heavy
Le Pupille, Micante
Caparzo, Brunello di Montalcino

Big Eye Hawaiian Ahi Tuna Tartare with Peppered Teriyaki Tuna Pastrami,
Eel Syrup, Oregon Wasabi, Ebony Caviar & Sesame Crisps
Colorado Springs Chorale 2005 Chefs' Gala
1st Place, Appetizers, James W. Davis, Jr. of The Blue Star
We did not include the recipe for this tapa because it takes 4 days to prepare.

Mixed Greens with Dried Fruit Cambozola Roulade, Rhubarb Compote and Currant Port Vinaigrette

Warm Cabbage with Prosciutto Vinaigrette

Stuffed Prince Edward Island Mussels

Red Leaf Lettuce and Asparagus Bundles with Raspberry Vinaigrette

Almond Rosemary Crusted Salmon with Saffron Rice

Jamaica Jerk Conch Chowder

Tito Puente Tilapia Tacos with Regina's Black Beans, Fruity Guacamole, and Green Rice

Grilled Lamb with Pine Nut Compound Butter

Poached Ahi Sashimi with Cucumber Salad

Cuban Beef on Sugar Cane Skewers

Wild Mushroom Loops with Asparagus and Red Burgundy Gastrique

Bocconcini Caprese Salad

Gorgonzola Beef Tips with House Mashers

Thai Duck with Sugar Snap Peas

Corleone

Chocolate Bread Pudding with Tuaca Caramel and French Crème

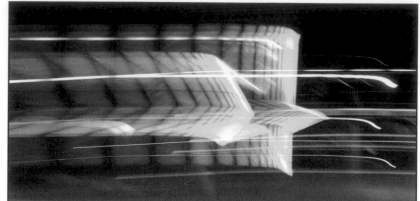

Sides

House Mashers

The Rice Page

Corn Confetti

Fruity Guacamole

Regina's Black Beans

Pico de Gallo

House Mashers

These mashed potatoes should come with a warning from the American Heart Association. The cream cheese and heavy cream make these among the smoothest, yummiest spuds on earth. This side dish is terrific with meat dishes. Rumor has it that Joseph Coleman, the Blue Star owner, perfected this recipe himself.

Time:
30 minutes

3 cups medium red potatoes, well-
　　washed with skin on, quartered
1 teaspoon and a pinch salt
1 tablespoon butter
2/3 cup leeks, finely chopped
2 tablespoons heavy cream
2 tablespoons cream cheese
1/2 teaspoon granulated garlic
salt and pepper to taste

Medium Red Potatoes

Place potatoes in pot and add enough water to cover them. Add a pinch of salt and boil until tender. Sweat leeks in butter, add cream, and scald the mixture. Reserve.

Drain cooked potatoes and place in mixer or heavy bowl if you are using a hand masher. Add hot cream mixture, cream cheese, 1 teaspoon salt, garlic granules, pepper (we like to be heavy on the pepper). Blend until smooth.

Sticky Rice

If you have a rice steamer, you can make sticky rice in it using the manufacturer's directions. Here is how to make it on the stove. We use this recipe with Poached Ahi Sashimi with Cucumber Salad (p. 45-46).

Time:
30 minutes

Makes
2 cups

1 cup Calrose rice
1-1/2 cups water

Rinse the rice in cold water 3 times. Strain it carefully, making sure all the liquid is out. Bring the rice and water to a boil. Cover and simmer on a low heat for 15 minutes. Do not stir.

Green Rice

Time:
30 minutes

Makes
2 cups

Cilantro gives this rice a bit of tang and color. It is a nice alternative to Spanish rice in Mexican-inspired dishes; we use it in with Tito Puente Tilapia Tacos (p. 44).

1 cup jasmine rice
1 -3/4 cups water
salt to taste
1/2 bunch cilantro
1 tablespoon light oil

Boil the jasmine rice in the water with the salt. Turn down heat and simmer until all the water is absorbed, about 20 minutes. Purée the cilantro and oil in a food processor. Toss the purée with the rice, being careful not to break the grains.

The Rice Page

Saffron Rice

A light side dish, saffron rice adds color and complements many Blue Star entrées without weighing them down.

Time:
30 minutes

Makes
2 cups

1 cup Uncle Ben's Converted Rice
1-3/4 cups water
1/2 carrot, finely diced
1 stalk celery, finely diced
1/4 onion, finely diced
2 tablespoons unsalted butter
1/2 pinch of saffron
salt to taste

In the sauce pan, sauté vegetables in butter until the onions are translucent.

Add rice and stir for 2 or 3 minutes so that you brown, but not burn, the rice. Have the water near at hand. As soon as the rice is a little brown, add 1-1/2 cups of water and bring to a boil.

Dissolve the saffron in 1/4 cup of water. Once the rice and vegetable mixture is boiling, add the saffron water, stir, and simmer covered for 20 minutes over low heat.

Corn Confetti

This is a sweet, hot, and colorful side dish. It is an ingredient in Laughing Lab Beef Chili (p. 56) and complements Tito Puente Tilapia Tacos (p.44), Cuban Beef Skewers (p. 9), and Mojo Marinated Chicken Quesadilla (p.10). It is also great with chips as an alternative to salsa.

Time:
30 minutes

Makes
2 cups

2 cups corn kernels

2 tablespoons olive oil

2 tablespoons red onion, finely
    chopped

2 tablespoons fresh cilantro, chopped

1 tablespoon jalapeño pepper,
    seeded and diced

Salt and pepper to taste

Mix the oil and corn and roast in a 350° oven until golden brown. This can take a while if the corn is frozen. The roasting brings out the sweetness of the corn. Combine corn with the remaining ingredients. Refrigerate until ready to serve.

Chef's note: You can roast whole ears of corn on the grill, leaving the shucks on. Then cut the kernels from the cob.

Fruity Guacamole

Time:
20 minutes

When avocados are plentiful, this is the side dish to make. Its bright colors and light texture make a beautiful variation that surprises diners with bits of peach and pomegranate seeds. This recipe is inspired by the culinary inventions of Peggy Taylor. We use the recipe as a side dish for Tito Puente Tilapia Tacos (p.44) and Mojo Marinated Chicken Quesadillas (p.10).

Makes 1-1/2
cups

2 avocados, halved and then diced

1 very firm peach, peeled and diced

1/2 red onion, finely diced,

1/4 cup pomegranate seeds

4 teaspoons lime juice

salt and pepper, to taste

SERVES 4

Chef's note: If peaches are unavailable, try another firm fruit. Have fun with it.

Combine the avocado and peach; add onion and pomegranate seeds. Stir gently to leave whole bits of avocado. Add lime juice. Salt and pepper to taste. Serve as a side with just about any Caribbean or Mexican entrée. Serve as a salad with organic greens and mango slices.

Regina's Black Beans

This Cuban staple is a simple and flavorful complement to many, many entrées. We use it with Tito Puente Tilapia Tacos (p.44). Who's Regina? She was Molly's college roommate, a native Cuban who introduced her to the wonders of garlic, guava, and Caribbean cookery.

Time:
Overnight
to soak the
beans,
2 hours
to cook

SERVES 4

2 cups dried black beans
water to cover
4 tablespoons duck fat* or olive oil
1 medium red onion, chopped
1 red pepper, chopped

1 tablespoon garlic, minced
1 bay leaf
1 teaspoon salt
salt and pepper to taste

*Duck fat lends a terrific flavor to these beans. You can buy some or reserve the fat from the Thai Duck recipe (p. 53). Stick to olive oil for the vegetarians in the house.

Soak the beans in a pot of water over night. Add more water if you need to.

In a sauce pan, melt the duck fat or heat the oil. Sweat the onion, pepper, and garlic. Add the soaked, drained beans and bay leaf. Add water until the beans are covered by 2 inches of water and add the salt. Bring the beans to a boil. Reduce the heat and slow boil until the beans are tender, about 1-1/2 hours. Add salt and pepper to taste.

Pico de Gallo

A fresh addition to Mexican-style dishes, this is easy to make and a simple pleasure to eat. We mention it as a side dish with *Mojo Marinated Chicken Quesadillas (p.10)* and *Tito Puente Tilapia Tacos (p.44)*. A batch of this pico de gallo will store in the refrigerator for a good three or four days.

Time:
15 minutes

Makes
1/2 cup

1 nice-sized tomato, small diced
2 tablespoon red onion, finely diced
4 tablespoons fresh cilantro, chopped
1 teaspoon garlic, chopped
1 tablespoon lime juice
salt and pepper to taste

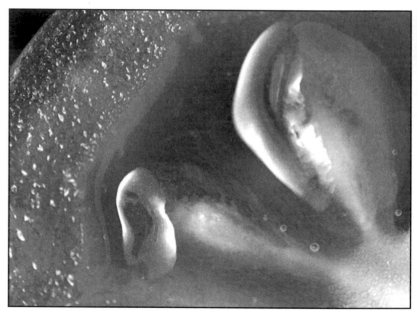

Tomato

Most of the work for this recipe will be at the cutting board. The idea is to cut up the ingredients so that they create a consistent, refined texture. Combine ingredients in a bowl. Refrigerate.

Desserts

Chocolate Bread Pudding with Tuaca Caramel

Banana Death

Chocolate Espresso Lava Cake with
Raspberry Syrup

Corleone

Chocolate Cheesecake

Buttermilk Brûlée

Tuaca Caramel

French Crème

Gingerbread Cake with Raspberry Salsa and Whipped Ginger Cream

Chocolate Bread Pudding
with Tuaca Caramel

This simple and decadent variation of an old-fashioned theme always brings applause. Joseph Coleman, the Blue Star owner, has been known to eat entire pans of this dessert. See picture on page 72. Plan on requests for second helpings.

Time:
1 hour

Makes
2 helpings
for 4

1 loaf of chocolate bread, a little stale if possible

3 eggs

1 cup sugar

2-1/2 cups half-and-half

1 tablespoon vanilla

1/4 pound unsalted butter

Preheat oven to 350°.

Cut bread in 3/8 " slices. Blend eggs, sugar, half-and-half, and vanilla. Use a little of the butter to grease a 9 x 9 inch baking dish. Dip each slice of bread in wet mixture and layer in the pan until all the bread is used. Pour any remaining wet mixture on the top. Using your hands, press down on the bread. Then top with remaining butter cut in slices. Cover with foil and bake for 40 minutes. Uncover and bake for an additional 15 minutes. Let stand for 10 minutes before serving.

Garnish with fruit and a dollop of French Crème (p.89), and drizzle with tuaca caramel (p.89).

Fonseca Bin 27
Grahams Vintage Port

Banana Death

As the name implies, this dessert is decadently over the top. Rich, heavy, creamy, sweet, tasty, and lovely. Reminiscent of Bananas Foster, this is definitely something to save room for.

Time:
20 minutes

4 bananas sliced in to 1/4 inch coins
1 tablespoon butter
1-1/2 oz. Myers 's Rum
1-1/2 oz. banana liqueur
1 cup tuaca caramel sauce (p.89)
1/4 cup shaves of white chocolate
1/4 cup shaves of dark chocolate
4 large scoops of Country Vanilla ice cream
4 sprigs of fresh mint

Chef's note: We use Colorado City Creamery ice cream for our desserts.

Sauté banana slices in butter for 15 seconds. Deglaze sauté pan with rum and banana liqueur. Add caramel sauce and mix. Put one scoop of ice cream in each of four bowls. Pour equal amounts of bananas and sauce over each scoop of ice cream. Sprinkle with shaves of white and dark chocolate. Garnish with sprig of mint.

Seppelt Tawny Port from Australia
Grahams 20 Year Tawny

Chocolate Espresso Lava Cake

Prepare yourself for the gasps as your diners find the molten chocolate and raspberry ganache filling. Depending on the size of your baking cups, this recipe makes 6 cakes.

This is a four-part recipe. We suggest starting with the ganache filling. If you prepare this dessert in the order suggested here, the whole endeavor will take about 1-1/2 hours.

Time:
90 minutes
Equipment:
5-ounce baking cups;
Muffin tins, or oven
proof ramekins.

Serves 6

Part one: Ganache filling
(40 minutes plus 20 minutes cooling)

2 ounces dark chocolate
    (weight measure)
2 teaspoons butter, salted
    or unsalted

1 tablespoon raspberry liqueur
1 egg yolk
4-1/2 teaspoons sugar
4-1/2 teaspoons cream

In a double boiler, melt the chocolate and butter. Add the liqueur.

In a bowl, whip the egg yolks and sugar until they form very stiff peaks. In a small sauce pan, scald the cream. Slowly whisk the hot cream into the egg yolk and sugar mixture. The idea is to temper the eggs, but not cook them. Whisk continually until the mixture covers the back of a spoon, about a minute.

Fold the cream, sugar, and yolks mixture into the chocolate, butter, and liqueur mixture. Pour this into the bottom of a small baking pan and refrigerate. It will be set up in 20 minutes.

While the ganache is setting up, start the cakes.

Part two: Cake batter
(20 minutes plus 15 minutes baking):

10 ounces of dark chocolate (weight measure)
1/3 cup of butter, salted or unsalted
2 tablespoons of espresso
7 egg yolks

1/4 cup and 1 tablespoon granulated sugar
1/8 teaspoon of pure vanilla extract
1 tablespoon all purpose flour
spray vegetable cooking oil

Preheat oven to 350°.
Place the chocolate, butter, and espresso in the top of a heated double boiler until the chocolate melts and is smooth.

In a separate bowl, place egg yolks, granulated sugar, vanilla, and flour. Blend at a high speed until the batter forms ribbons when you lift the beaters. The ribbons will then melt back into the yolks.

Fold the chocolate mixture into the yolk mixture with a spatula; when you see a little marbling, it is just right.

Spray oil on the inside of five, 5-ounce baking cups. Fill each cup half way with the batter. Then put a 3/4-inch ball of cooled ganache in the middle of the cup, and then fill the cups with batter.

Bake for 15 to 18 minutes, cool completely and flip out of baking cups.

While the cakes are baking, start the raspberry syrup.

Part three: Raspberry syrup
(25 minutes)

1/2 cup frozen raspberries
6 tablespoons of sugar

Combine berries and sugar in a saucepan over a low heat. Cook until the berries melt and the sugar dissolves. Reduce by 1/3 very slowly, about 20 minutes. Strain through a fine strainer or cheese cloth. Makes 1/3 cup of syrup.

Part four: Topping

4 scoops French Silk Chocolate ice cream

When you are ready to serve this dessert, heat the cakes in a 500° oven for 4 or 5 minutes; this makes the ganache molten in the middle. Top with French Silk Chocolate Ice Cream, and drizzle with raspberry syrup.

Imperial Stout
A big dessert needs a big stout. The Imperial stout is loaded with intense roast, coffee, chocolate and fruit notes, which will mingle with the chocolate and counter the cake's rich filling. The warming effect of this beer's hefty alcohol content will finish a meal in style.
Rogue Shakespeare Stout, Rogue Ales, Oregon
Samuel Smith Imperial Stout, The Old Brewery at Tadcaster, England

Corleone

Like watching old Warner Brothers cartoons with the kids on Saturday morning, this crusted ice cream dessert is a delightful trip back to childhood. Just as classical music was in the background as Bugs outwitted Elmer yet again, this dessert mixes in the grown-up flavors of nutmeg and cinnamon. This recipe is inspired by Timothy Creehan, Certified Executive Chef. See page 72 for a picture.

Time:
30 minutes

SERVES 4

1/3 cup almonds, sliced

1/3 cup walnut pieces

2 tablespoons pecan pieces

3 tablespoons white chocolate, chopped

3 tablespoons dark chocolate, chopped

3/4 teaspoon nutmeg

1 teaspoon cinnamon

1/2 cup graham cracker crumbs

4 scoops Country Vanilla ice cream

1/2 cup honey

4 sprigs mint

Toast the nuts in a 350° oven (a toaster oven works well) until golden brown, about 7 minutes.
In a food processor, blend the almonds, walnuts, pecans, white and dark chocolate, nutmeg, cinnamon, and graham cracker crumbs. Mix until the texture is fairly fine but still has some little chunks in it.

Roll each scoop of ice cream in the mixture until completely coated. Place scoops in a bowls or wine glasses, drizzle each with about 2 tablespoons of honey and garnish with a sprig of mint.

Ice cream is always tough to match. **Cream Sherry** is a good date.
For something more extravagant, **Merryvale** makes a dessert wine called "**Antigua**," made in the Port style from Muscat grapes and aged for 10 years in a barrel to give it a good nutty, vanilla flavoring.

Chocolate Cheesecake

This dessert is a sensation; it is fast to make and almost as fast to disappear. Diners rave about this cheesecake's rich flavor and texture. For a beautiful color contrast (and to add just a few calories), serve with 1 tablespoon of French Crème (p. 89) on each serving.

Time:
40 minutes to prepare plus 3 hours or overnight for the cake to set.
Equipment:
Spring form baking pan

Serves 12

Crust
Spray oil or 1 tablespoon vegetable oil
1 cup graham cracker crumbs
1/8 cup sugar
1/4 cup melted butter

Filling
22 ounces cream cheese (almost 3, 8-ounce packages)
2/3 cup sugar
1/2 cup soft unsalted butter
16 ounces semi-sweet chocolate, melted
1-1/4 cup whipping cream, not whipped

Preheat oven to 350°.
Make the crust first so it can cool while you make the filling. Coat the sides and bottom of the spring form pan with spray oil or with vegetable oil. Combine the graham cracker crumbs, sugar, and butter. Press the mixture into the bottom only of the spring form pan. Bake for 5 minutes. Remove from oven and allow to cool.

This filling needs no baking! Beat the cream cheese and sugar until smooth. Then add soft butter and mix by hand or with a mixer. Add the melted chocolate and blend. In a separate bowl, whip the whipping cream until it peaks and add 2 cups of it to the filling mixture. Blend the entire filling mixture until smooth.

Pour the filling into the crust and refrigerate. Allow to set for at least three hours before serving. Run a knife around the inside of the pan to make it easier to remove the spring form pan. Cut into as many pieces as you wish.

While the cheesecake is setting, you can make the French Crème topping (p. 89); you will need a cup or so of topping. In fact, if you have 2 ounces of cream cheese left over when you make this cheesecake, you will have just enough to make the French Crème, too.

Stout
While you can serve Guinness with this dish, the American craft-brewed stouts have a fuller body, which better complements the dessert's sweetness. These beers still have plenty of roast, bitter, and coffee flavors to truly bring out the rich flavor of the cheesecake. You may never have coffee with dessert again!
Out of Bounds Stout, Avery Brewing, Colorado
Sierra Nevada Stout, Sierra Nevada Brewing, California

Buttermilk Brûlée

Everyone remembers the best crème brûlée they ever had, and it is tough to compete with special memories. Not to be deterred, James Davis devised this tasty variation on a familiar theme. It could be your new favorite, especially when all you hear is the click, click, clank of spoons in the bottoms of the custard cups.

Time:
2 1/2 hours,
30 minutes,
active
Equipment:
5-ounce baking or
custard cups
A very hot
broiler or a culinary
butane torch

SERVES 4

2 egg yolks
2 whole eggs
1/3 cup sugar
1-1/2 cups half and half
1/2 cup buttermilk

1/2 teaspoon vanilla
1 tablespoon turbinado
  sugar

Preheat oven to 250°.

Combine egg yolks, whole eggs, sugar, half-and-half, buttermilk, and vanilla; whisk until completely blended. Let the mixture rest until all the air bubbles settle out. Fill four custard cups 7/8 full. Place the custard cups in a baking dish large enough to hold them all. Fill the dish with water to the rims of the custard cups. Cover the whole thing with aluminum foil.

Bake at 250° for 1-3/4 to 2 hours. You can tell the custard is done when it jiggles in the middle just a little bit. Remove the custard cups from the water bath and let cool. Refrigerate until ready to serve.

Just before serving, sprinkle each cup with turbinado sugar, and, using either a broiler or a culinary butane torch, carmelize the sugar. Let the sugar cool enough to cover the custard with a shell.

Writer's note: A torch is a much better way to accomplish the ice-like layer of sugar on the brûlée. A broiler takes too long and heats the custard, which can really change its texture for the worse.

Nothing goes better with Brûlée than a **Tawny Port.** For an inexpensive option, try **Australian Seppelt, Penfolds, and Galway Pipe.** **Grahams 20 year Tawny from Portugal**, however, is simply one of the best ever.

Tuaca Caramel Sauce

This is a great deal of very careful work and can go wrong easily. To make it is an accomplishment to be proud of, and it is ever so tasty. It is a perfect topping for Chocolate Bread Pudding (p.82) and a crucial ingredient for Banana Death (p. 83).

3/4 cup cream
3/4 cup sugar

1/4 cup tuaca, an Italian liqueur

It seems easy enough to say "caramelize sugar," but this can be quite a process. In the heavy-bottomed pan, heat the sugar over a medium heat. If you use a gas stove, be sure that the flames are not hitting the sides of the pan. Eventually, the sugar will turn amber and start sticking together. Start scraping the amber sugar away from the bottom so that it doesn't burn. Handle it as little as possible; do not stir. As the sugar liquefies, keep moving it around. When all the sugar is liquid, slowly, slowly stir in the cream. Be careful when adding the cream; steam billows forth quickly. Stir in tuaca. If you have a gas stove, be careful of flames emerging when stirring in the liqueur.

Chef's note: You can buy commercial caramel sauce and add 3 tablespoons of tuaca per cup of caramel. It is easier, but not nearly as good.

Time:
45 minutes
(approx.)

Makes
1-1/2 cup

French Crème

What a dessert topping ought to be! Rich, luscious, and flavorful. Use this to top berries for a simple but decadent dessert. French crème has a slightly tart flavor that complements sweet desserts such as Chocolate Cheesecake (p. 87).

Time:
20 minutes
Equipment: mixer

Makes 4 cups

1-1/2 cups whipping cream
1/2 cup powdered sugar
1 teaspoon vanilla extract

6 ounces cream cheese, softened
3/4 cup sour cream

In medium mixing bowl, combine whipping cream, sugar, and vanilla. Whip this mixture at a high speed until the whipping cream has soft peaks. In another bowl, blend the cream cheese and sour cream at a medium speed. Then fold the cream cheese and sour cream into the whipping cream mixture. Refrigerate until ready to use.

Chef's note: One batch of this recipe will make enough to put a 1/4 to 1/3 cup topping on each of 12 slices of cheese cake. If you want less, cut the recipe accordingly. But what's wrong with a little leftover for dabbing on fresh berries in a day or two?

Gingerbread Cake
with Raspberry Salsa and Whipped Ginger Cream

Time:
1 hour

We thank Dave Gordon for this recipe that moves gingerbread into the ranks of classy desserts. This is rich, moist, flavorful, and beautiful. It is especially welcome to those who prefer not to eat chocolate.

SERVES 4

Gingerbread

Oil and flour to prepare
   baking pan

2 cups flour

1/2 cup golden brown sugar

1 tablespoon ground ginger

1-1/2 teaspoons baking soda

1-1/2 teaspoons salt

1/4 teaspoon ground nutmeg

1/4 teaspoon ground cinnamon

1/2 cup molasses

6 tablespoons vegetable oil

1/2 cup applesauce

1 egg

1/2 cup boiling water

Preheat oven to 350°.
Oil the baking pan and coat with a teaspoon or less of flour. Whisk together flour, sugar, ginger, baking soda, salt, nutmeg, and cinnamon in a medium bowl. In a large bowl, whisk together molasses, oil, applesauce, and egg until blended. Add dry ingredients and stir until well-blended. Whisk in 1/2 cup of boiling water. Pour into 9 x 9 inch baking pan. Bake for about 15 minutes, but keep your eye on it because this recipe is much better a little moist. Let cool for 10 minutes and then turn the cake out of the pan. While the cake is baking, make the salsa and whipped cream.

Red Raspberry Salsa
Makes 1 cup
3/4 cup fresh raspberries
1/4 cup sugar
1/8 cup framboise

Time:
5 minutes

Red Raspberries

Purée 1/2 cup of red raspberries with sugar and framboise.
Add the remaining whole berries and stir.

Ginger Whipped Cream
Makes 3/4 cup

Time:
10 minutes

1 tablespoon crystallized ginger
1/2 cup whipping cream
1/2 teaspoon vanilla

Grind or finely chop the ginger. Whip vanilla and cream to stiff peaks. Fold in ginger. This topping will hold its peaks for two days.

Place a 2" x 2" square of gingerbread on each plate. Drizzle with raspberry salsa and top with whipping cream. Top with a whole raspberry from the salsa.

Clocktower Tawny Port from Australia
Taylor 10 Year Tawny

Leo, James, and St. Francis

Gathering Ingredients

The ingredients listed here may seem hard to find, so we listed what they are and the kind of store we found them in. Only three items were really hard to locate: lamb loins, conch, and tasso ham. Please note that most stores, especially our sponsors, will happily special order items for you if they don't have them in stock.

Callebaut white chocolate (a fine brand of high fat, white chocolate) – gourmet food stores and grocery stores

Calrose rice (short-grain, white rice good for sticky rice) - Asian and specialty stores

Chile paste (Chinese hot pepper paste) - grocery, gourmet, and Asian specialty stores

Chipotle pepper purée (chipotle pepper ground up in vinegar or water) – grocery, gourmet, and Mexican specialty stores

Chocolate bread – specialty bakeries and gourmet food stores

Conch – special order at gourmet food stores

Cream of coconut (very sweet, almost solid coconut cream) – Coco Lopez is the most common brand; you'll find it in grocery and gourmet stores.

Demi glace (reduced veal or beef stock) – gourmet and specialty stores

Duck breasts – gourmet and specialty stores

Duck fat – gourmet and specialty stores

Framboise (raspberry liqueur) – liquor stores

Jamaican jerk seasoning (combination of Caribbean herbs and seasoning) – gourmet and grocery stores

Jasmine rice (fragrant, white rice) – grocery and specialty stores

Kaffir lime leaves (Glossy, dark green leaves with a unique double shape that looks like two leaves joined end to end. Dried kaffir lime rind and leaves have a flora-citrus aroma. Fresh leaves have more aroma and are sometimes available.) – gourmet and Asian specialty stores

Lamb loins – stores with extensive, gourmet meat counters or special order at grocery stores

Mae Ploy sauce (Thai sweet chile sauce) - grocery, gourmet, and Asian specialty stores

Maggi sauce (seasoning sauce) – grocery and gourmet stores

Mango purée – gourmet stores carry mango purée, but you can buy a mango at a grocery store and purée it yourself.

Mirin (low alcohol rice wine from Japan) – grocery and Asian specialty stores.

Mushroom soy sauce (soy sauce with mushroom flavoring) – grocery, natural food, gourmet, and Asian specialty stores

Mussels (fresh or frozen) – grocery and gourmet stores with seafood sections

Nam pla (salty, fermented Thai fish sauce with an extremely pungent odor) – gourmet and Asian specialty stores

Pepperoncini peppers (Italian pickled hot peppers) – grocery and gourmet stores

Pickled ginger (thin slices of ginger in pickling brine) – gourmet and Asian specialty stores

Pomegranate seeds (the little, bright red juice sacks inside the pomegranate fruit) – gourmet grocery stores when in season, September through January. You can freeze pomegranate seeds for later use.

Quail - gourmet stores with an extensive poultry section or special order at grocery stores

Queso blanco (Mexican white cheese) – grocery or Mexican specialty stores

Sambal (Indonesian, Malaysian and southern Indian multipurpose, hot condiment that has as its base a mixture of chiles, brown sugar, and salt. Has many variations) - gourmet and Asian specialty stores

Srirachi paste (Thai chile and garlic paste) – gourmet and Asian specialty stores

Su (mild, slightly sweet Japanese rice vinegar) – gourmet and Asian specialty stores

Sweet Thai chile sauce (Mae Ploy is a popular brand of this sauce that is just as the name suggests) – grocery, gourmet, and Asian specialty stores

Tahini (nut butter made of sesame seeds) - grocery, gourmet, and natural food stores

Tamarind paste (strong-flavored sweet and sour paste from inside tamarind seed pods) – Grocery stores carry tamarind beans that you can boil to get the paste out from around the seeds; gourmet, Asian, and East Indian specialty stores carry the paste.

Tasso ham (Cajun spicy ham) – hard to find even at specialty stores; you'll have best luck near Mardi Gras time. If you can't find it and you want to make the Prince Edward Island Stuffed Mussels, sauté some andouille sausage (grocery and gourmet stores) to give the recipe some Cajun flavor.

Vanilla paste – grocery and specialty stores

Veal bones – grocery store and butcher

Vinegars (balsamic, white balsamic, currant, champagne, raspberry) – grocery and specialty stores

Wasabi (Japanese, green-colored condiment with a sharp, pungent, fiery flavor; a.k.a., Japanese horseradish) – specialty stores carry wasabi in tubes or as a powder; fresh wasabi is tough to find.

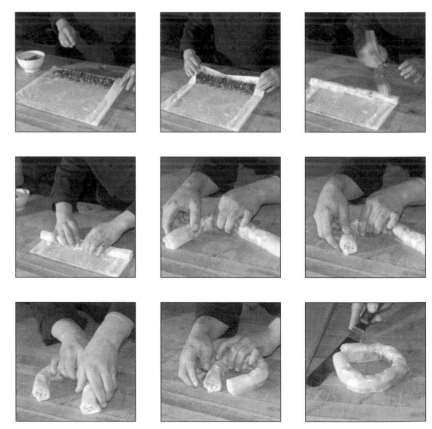

Rolling Mushroom Loops, recipe on page 60.

Glossary of Cooking terms

We've included a few definitions of cooking terms we use in *The Blue Star Cookbook: Try This at Home.* Several kitchen testers asked us what the difference was among beating, blending, folding, whipping, and so on. We hope these definitions clear the air.

Bard: To tie fat, such as bacon or fatback, around lean meats to prevent their drying out while cooking. The barding fat bastes the meat while it cooks, thereby retaining moisture and adding flavor.

Beat: To beat is to stir rapidly in a circular motion. Generally, 100 strokes by hand equals about 1 minute by electric mixer.

Blend: To mix two or more ingredients together with a spoon, beater, or electric blender only as long as it takes to combine the ingredients.

Caramelize: To heat sugar until it liquefies and becomes a clear syrup ranging in color from golden to dark brown. In the case of desserts, for example, granulated or brown sugar is sprinkled on top of food and placed under a heat source, such as a broiler or a cooking torch, until the sugar melts, such as in the recipe for *Buttermilk Brûlée.*

When talking about caramelizing onions, though, you slowly sweat the onions to cook all the sugar out of them. They then turn brown, as in the recipe for Warlock Onions.

Chiffonnade (shihf-uh-NAHD): Literally translated, this word means "made of rags." In the kitchen, we mean cut up vegetables or herbs into thin strips or shreds. See picture on page 107.

Chinois (SHEEN-wah): A chinois is a metal, conical sieve with an extremely fine mesh used for puréeing or straining. The mesh is so fine that a spoon or pestle must be used to press the food through it.

Combine: To mix two or more ingredients together until they do not separate. See "blend" above.

Debeard: A beard is the common name for the silky, hairlike filaments that bivalves (such as oysters and mussels) use to attach themselves to rocks, piers, and so on. The beard is not attractive or tasty. If you see a beard, it must be trimmed before the shellfish is prepared, hence debearding.

Deglaze: After food (usually meat) has been sautéed and the food and excess fat removed from the pan, deglazing is done by heating a small amount of liquid (wine or stock) in the pan and stirring to loosen browned bits of food (the fond) on the bottom. This new liquid is then used to make a sauce or gravy.

Dépouillage (DAY-pwee-ahj): Skimming the fat and impurities off of the surface of a stock or soup.

Emulsify: To mix one liquid with another with which it cannot normally combine smoothly — oil and water, for example. Emulsifying is done by slowly (sometimes drop-by-drop) adding one ingredient to another while at the same time mixing rapidly. This disperses and suspends minute droplets of one liquid throughout the other. Emulsified mixtures are usually thick and satiny in texture. We use "emulsify" in the recipes for salad dressings, Chipotle Aioli, and James Davis's Hollandaise.

Fold: A technique used to gently combine a light, airy mixture (such as beaten egg whites) with a heavier mixture (such as whipped cream or custard). The lighter mixture is placed on top of the heavier one in a large bowl. Starting at the back of the bowl, a rubber spatula is used to cut down vertically through the two mixtures, across the bottom of the bowl and up the nearest side. The bowl is rotated a quarter turn with each series of strokes. This down-across-up-and-over motion gently turns the mixtures over on top of each other, combining them in the process.

Julienne (joo-lee-EHN): To cut food into very thin strips, like matchsticks.

Mignonette (meen-yawn-NEHT): This term has several meanings, but for our purpose, it refers to coarsely ground or chopped peppercorns.

Render: To melt animal fat over low heat so that it separates from any connective pieces of tissue which, during rendering, turn brown and crisp and are generally referred to as cracklings. The resulting clear fat is then strained through a paper filter or fine cheesecloth to remove any dark particles.

Scald: A cooking technique whereby a liquid is heated to just below the boiling point. Scald is also used to describe plunging food such as tomatoes or peaches into boiling water in order to loosen their skin and facilitate peeling. Also referred to as "blanching."

Sweat: A technique by which ingredients, particularly vegetables, are cooked in a small amount of fat over low heat. With this method, the ingredients soften without browning and cook in their own juices.

Whip: To beat ingredients, such as egg whites or cream, thereby incorporating air into them and increasing their volume until they are light and fluffy.

Chopping Onions

Old enough to know.
TWENTY-FOUR YEARS
OF EDUCATING PALATES IN COLORADO SPRINGS!

At COALTRAIN, we know food...and the wines and beers that go with it. Our award-winning staff can create a food-and-drink match made in heaven – just for you – from among the thousands of bottles in our inventory.

KNOWLEDGE • EXPERIENCE • SERVICE • PASSION • INTEGRITY

That's **COALTRAIN**

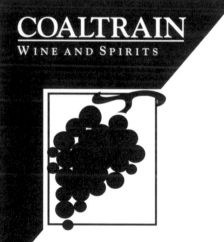

COALTRAIN
WINE AND SPIRITS

330 W. Uintah Street
Colorado Springs, CO 80905
719-475-9700

Beer and Wine Index

Beers

Ale, Scottish
Laughing Lab Scottish Ale, Bristol Brewing (Colorado), 56
Golden Ale, Belgium
La Chouffe, Brasserie D'Achouffe (Belgium), 5
Pranqster Belgian style Golden Ale, North Coast Brewing (Cal.), 5
Pale Ale, American-style
Liberty Ale, Anchor Brewing, 48
Wet Mountain IPA, Il Vicino Brewing (New Mexico & Colorado), 48
Pilsner, European-style
Blue Paddle Pilsner, New Belgium Brewing (Colorado), 31
Pilsner Urquell, SAB Miller (Czech Bohemia), 31
Stout
Out of Bounds Stout, Avery Brewing (Colorado), 87
Rogue Shakespeare Stout, Rogue Ales (Oregon), 85
Samuel Smith Imperial Stout, The Old Brewery at Tadcaster (England), 85
Sierra Nevada Stout, Sierra Nevada Brewing (California), 87
Wheat Beer, Bavarian
Schneider Weiss, G. Schneider & Sohn (Germany), 10
Tabernash Weiss, Left Hand/Tabernash Brewery (Colorado), 10
Wheat Beer, Belgium
Allagash White, Allagash Brewing (Maine), 44
Hoegaarden White, Hoegaarden (Belgium), 44

Red Wines

Barbaresco
Produttori del Barbaresco, Barbaresco, Langhe (Italy), 20
Barbera d'Alba
Gagliardo (Italy), 17
Beaujolais
Georges DuBoeuf, "Jean Descombes" (France), 20
Louis Jadot (France), 19
Brunello
Caparzo, Brunello di Montalcino (Italy), 64
Cabernet Sauvignon
Howell Mountain (California), 57
Martin Ray "Angeline" (California), 55
Penfolds Bin 707 (Australia), 55
Steltzner, Stag Leaps District (California), 59
Charbono
Bonny Doon Vineyard Ca' del Solo "La Farfalla" (California), 17

Chianti
La Massa "Giorgio Primo" (Italy), 52
Rodano Chianti Classico Riserva (Italy), 42
Villa Guilia "Alaura" (Italy), 52
Cotes du Rhone
Perrin (France), 57
Malbec
Trapiche Malbec Oak Cask (Argentina), 58
Médoc
Domaine Lafite-Rothschild, Pauillac (France), 59
Merlot
Heron Merlot, Vin de Pays (France), 61
Naoussa
Ktima Karyda (Greece), 62
Pinot Noir
Acacia Carneros (California), 2
Archery Summit (Oregon), 53
Bethel Heights (Oregon), 50
Bouchard Old Vines (France), 2
David Bruce, Central Coast (California), 53
Saintsbury "Garnet" (California), 19
Vavasour "Dashwood" (New Zealand), 42
Port
Clocktower Tawny (Australia), 91
Fonseca Bin 27 (Portugal), 82
Galway Pipe Tawny (Australia), 88
Grahams 20 Year Tawny (Portugal), 83, 88
Grahams Vintage (Portugal), 82
Penfolds Tawny (Australia), 88
Seppelt Tawny (Australia), 83, 88
Taylor 10 Year Tawny (Portugal), 91
Saint George
Domaine Skouras (Greece), 62
Sangiovese blend (Super Tuscans)
Castellare di Castellina, I Sodi di San Niccolò (Italy), 61
Fattoria Le Pupille "Micante" (Italy), 64
Zinfandel
Robert Biale, "Monte Rosso" (California), 58
Renwood, Sierra Series (California), 9
Ridge (California), 9
Rosenblum (California), 9
Seghesio Old Vine (California), 9

Rosé Wines

Bruno Clair, Marsannay, (France), 50
Guigal (France), 30
Tablas Creek (Paso Robles, California) 13, 50
Renwood Syrah (California), 13, 50

Toad Hollow Pinot Noir Rosé (California), 15
Zaca Mesa (California), 15

Sherries and Dessert Wines

Amontillado, 27
Cream, 86
Dios Baco Fino (Spain), 6
Fino, 27
Merryvale Antigua (California), 86

Sparkling Wines

Seaview (Australia), 7
Segura Viudas, Brut Reserva (Spain), 12
Tattinger, La Francaise (France), 7

White Wines

Albariño
    Condes de Albarei (Spain), 3
    Morgadio (Spain), 29
Chardonnay
    Cartlidge and Brown (California), 49
    Landmark "Overlook" (California), 43
    Newton, Unfiltered (California), 49
Chenin Blanc
    MAN Vintners (South Africa), 46
Gewurztraminer
    Trimbach (France), 26
    Zind-Humbrecht (France), 26
Gruner Veltliner
    Nigl (Austria), 46
Marsanne
    Preston Ranch Vineyards (California), 12
Pinot Grigio
    Luna (California), 18
    Zenato (Italy), 18
Sauvignon Blanc
    Geisen (New Zealand), 3
    Napa Wine Company (California), 8
    Pascal Jolivet (France), 8
    Spring Mountain (California), 14
    Undurraga (Chile), 29
Soave Classico
    Guerrieri-Rizzardi (Italy), 14

Viognier
    Jewel (California), 43
Rioja
    Marquès de Cacéres (Spain), 30

The Cork

Blue Star Cookbook Index

Recipe titles appear in italics.
Bolded pages refer to recipe photographs.

A

Ahi sashimi, poached, 45–46, **69**
Aioli, chipotle, 38
Ale, Laughing Lab
    beef chili, 56
Almond Rosemary Crusted Salmon, 42, **68**
Appetizers. *See* Tapas
Asian-inspired dishes
    ahi sashimi, poached, 45–46, **69**
    coconut peanut shrimp satay, 6
    duck, Thai, 53, **71**
    shrimp cakes, Thai, 4–5
Asparagus
    bundles, with red leaf lettuce, 13, **67**
    wild mushroom loops, 60–61
Asparagus and Red Leaf Lettuce Salad, 13, **67**
Athena's Goat Cheese Terrine, 8
Avocado
    fruity guacamole, 78

B

Balsamic Vinaigrette, 24
Banana Death, 83
Banana dessert, with caramel and ice cream, 83
Barding, defined, 57, 97
Basil
    sun dried tomato pesto, 37
Beans
    black, Regina's, 79
    white, Tuscan, 51
Beef
    barding, about, 57
    chili, with Laughing Lab ale, 56
    Cuban, skewered, 9, **69**
    searing, about, 56
    steak au poivre, 58
    tenderloin fillet, stuffed, 57
    tips, with portobello and gorgonzola, 59, **70**

Beer
    onions, caramelized, 40
    recipe pairings
        about, xiii–xiv
        index to, 99–100
Bisques
    butternut, 27
Black beans, 79
Bocconcini Caprese Salad, 18, **70**
Bomb Sauce, 38
Bread crumb topping (persillade), 40
Bread pudding, chocolate, **72**, 82
Brie, and smoked salmon, en croûte, 2
Brûlée, buttermilk, 88
Burgundy
    gastrique, 61
Butter, pine nut
    recipe for, 54
    uses for, 55
Buttermilk brûlée, 88
Butternut Bisque, 27

C

Cabbage salad, warm, 20, **66**
Cajun dishes
    shrimp creole, Jimmy's, 47–48
Cakes
    chocolate espresso, 84–85
        ganache filling for, 84
    gingerbread, 90–91
Cambozola roulade, with dried fruit, 16
Caramel sauce, tuaca, 89
Caribbean-inspired dishes
    beef on sugar cane skewers, Cuban, 9
    black beans, Regina's, 79
    conch chowder, Jamaica jerk, 31, **68**
Carrot Cumin Soup, 30
Cheese
    brie en croûte, with salmon, 2
    cambozola roulade, with dried fruit, 16
    cream, in chocolate cheesecake, 87
    feta
        in Company Salad, 15
        in Greek pasta, 62
    goat
        lamb loin, 54

in moussaka, 63
terrine, 8
gorgonzola
portobello beef tips, 59
stuffed tenderloin fillet, 57
mozzarella, in salad, with tomatoes, 18, **70**
parmesan
crusted halibut, 43
in Tuscan white beans, 51
pecorino romano, in Tuscan white beans, 51
queso blanco, in chicken quesadillas, 10
regiano parmegiano
in Company Salad, 15
in tomato pesto, 37
Cheese Stuffed Poblano Pepper Wraps, 7
Cheesecake, chocolate, 87
Chef's Gala, **65**
Chicken
quesadillas, marinated in mojo sauce, 10
stock, 33
tortilla soup, with lime, 28–29
Chicken Lime Tortilla Soup, 28–29
Chicken Stock, 33
Chili, beef, with Laughing Lab ale, 56
Chipotle Aioli, 38
Chocolate
bread pudding, with caramel, **72**, 82
cake, with espresso, 84–85
cheesecake, 87
Chocolate Bread Pudding with Tuaca Caramel, **72**, 82
Chocolate Cheesecake, 87
Chocolate Espresso Lava Cake, 84
Chowders
Jamaica jerk conch, 31, **68**
Coconut Peanut Shrimp Satay, 6
Company Salad, 15
Compote, rhubarb, 17
Conch chowder, 31, **68**
Corleone, **72**, 86
Corn Confetti, 78
Corn salad, 78
Crab
cakes, 49
stuffed, in mushrooms, 50
Crab Stuffed Portobello Mushrooms, 50
Cream, whipped, ginger, 91
Crème brûlée, buttermilk, 88
Crème, French, 89

Creole, shrimp, 47–48
Crostini, herbed, 21
Croutons, homemade, 21
Cuban Beef on Sugar Cane Skewers, 9, **69**
Cuban-inspired dishes
beef on sugar cane skewers, 9, **69**
black beans, Regina's, 79
Currant Port Vinaigrette, 23
Custard. *See* Crème brûlée

D

Demi-Glace, veal, 36
Dépouillage, defined, 35, 97
Desserts
banana dessert, 83
bread pudding, chocolate, with caramel, **72**, 82
cake, chocolate espresso, 84–85
cheesecake, chocolate, 87
corleone, 86
crème brûlée, buttermilk, 88
ice cream
with banana and caramel, 86
crusted, **72**, 86
Difficulty ratings, about, xiii
Dressings. *See* Salad dressings
Duck, Thai, 53, **71**

E

Eggplant
moussaka, 63–64
Entrées
beef
chili, with Laughing Lab, 56
steak au poivre, 58
tenderloin fillet, stuffed, 57
tips, with portobello and gorgonzola, 59, **70**
duck, Thai, 53, **71**
fish
ahi sashimi, poached, 45–46, **69**
halibut, parmesan crusted, 43
salmon, almond rosemary, 42, **68**
tilapia tacos, 44, **68**
lamb loin, grilled, 55, **69**
quail, grilled, 52
shellfish
crab cakes, 49
crab stuffed portobello mushrooms, 50

shrimp creole, Jimmy's, 47–48
vegetarian
    moussaka, 63–64
    pasta, warm Greek, 62
    wild mushroom loops, 60–61
Equipment, kitchen
    for each recipe, about, xiii
    knives, xiv

F

Feta cheese
    cabbage salad, 20
    Greek pasta, 62
Filet mignon
    portobello gorgonzola beef tips, 59
Fish
    ahi sashimi, poached, 45–46, **69**
    halibut, parmesan crusted, 43
    salmon, almond rosemary, 42, **68**
    tilapia tacos, 44, **68**
Fond, defined, 56
French Crème, 89
Fruity Guacamole, 78

G

Game. *See* Quail
Ganache, chocolate and raspberry, 84
Gastrique, red burgundy, 61
Ginger
    gingerbread cake, 90
    whipped cream, 91
Ginger Whipped Cream, 91
Gingerbread Cake with Raspberry Salsa and Whipped Ginger Cream, 90–91
Glace de Viande, 36
Glossary of cooking terms, 97–98
Goat cheese, French-Style chèvre
    lamb loin, 54
    nutmeg-cinnamon, 63
    terrine, Athena's, 8
Gorgonzola
    and portobello beef tips, 59
    in stuffed tenderloin fillet, 57
Grapes
    champagne, chef's note, 43
    with parmesan crusted halibut, 43
Gravies, about, 36

Greek-inspired dishes
    goat cheese terrine, Athena's, 8
    moussaka, 63–64
    warm Greek pasta, 62
Green Rice, 77
Grilled foods
    beef, Cuban, skewered, 9
    beef tenderloin fillet, stuffed, 57
    "Bomb" sauce for, 38
    lamb loin, 55, **69**
    moussaka, 63–64
    quail, 51–52
Grilled Lamb Loin with Pine Nut Compound Butter, 54–55, **69**
Grilled Quail with Tuscan White Beans, 51–52
Guacamole, fruity, 78

H

Halibut, parmesan crusted, 43
Herbed Crostini, 21
Herbs, fresh v. dried, xiv
Hollandaise sauce, James Davis's, 39
House Mashers, 76

I

Ice cream
    with banana caramel dessert, 83
    chocolate silk, with chocolate espresso cake, 85
    crusted, **72**, 86
Indonesian-inspired dishes
    coconut peanut shrimp satay, 6
Ingredients, hard to find, 93–95
Institutional Salad, 14

J

Jamaica Jerk Conch Chowder, 31, **68**
Jamaican-inspired dishes
    conch chowder, 31
James Davis's Hollandaise Sauce, 39
Japanese-inspired dishes
    ahi sashimi, poached, 45–46
Just Warm Greek Pasta, 62

K

Knives, about, xiv

L

Lamb, grilled, with compound butter, 54–55, **69**
Laughing Lab Beef Chili, 56
Lettuce
    mixed greens, with bocconcini, 18, **70**
    mixed greens, with roulade, compote and vinaigrette, 16
    red leaf, and asparagus bundles, 13
    romaine, in "Institutional" salad, 14
Louisiana Crab Cakes, 49

M

Marinades
    "Bomb" sauce, 38
    "Mojo" sauce, 9
Mashers, house, 76
Meat. *See* Beef
Mexican-inspired dishes
    chicken quesadillas, marinated, 10
    chicken tortilla soup, with lime, 28–29
    fruity guacamole, 78
    pico de gallo, 80
    tacos, tilapia, 44, **68**
Mignonette, defined, 19, 98
Mixed greens with Dried Fruit Cambozola Roularde, Rhubarb Compote, and
        Currant Port Vinaigrette, 16, **66**
Mojo Marinated Chicken Quesadillas, 10
Mojo Sauce, 9
Moussaka Deconstructa, 63
Mozzarella balls salad, 18, **70**
Mushroom Stock, 37
Mushrooms
    porcini filling, 57
    portobello, stuffed with crab, 50
    stock, 37
    wild mushroom loops, 60–61, **70**
Mussels, stuffed, 3, **66**
Mutton. *See* Lamb

N

New York Strip
    portobello gorgonzola beef tips, 59
Nutmeg-cinnamon goat cheese, 63

O

Oils
    garlic-infused, for dipping, 3
    for sautéing, chef's note, 32
Onions
    caramelized, 40
    soup, Swiss, 26
    Vidalia, in spinach pine nut salad, 12
Orzo
    warm Greek pasta, 62

P

Parmegiano, regiano
    in Company Salad, 15
    tomato pesto, 37
Parmesan
    crusted halibut, 43
    Tuscan white beans, 51
Parmesan Crusted Halibut with Red Grapes, 43
Pasta, warm Greek, 62
Pastry, puff
    salmon and brie en croûte, 2
Peas, sugar snap, 53
Pecorino romano
    Tuscan white beans, 51
Pepper, black
    mignonette preparation, 19
    using to taste, in recipes, xiv
Peppercorns, types of, xiv
Peppers
    chipotle, aioli, 38
    poblano, cheese stuffed wraps, 7
Persillade, 40
Pesto, sun dried tomato, 37
Pico de Gallo, 80
Pine nuts
    compound butter, 54
    sun dried tomato pesto, 37
    Vidalia onion and spinach salad, 12
Poached Ahi Sashimi with Cucumber Salad 45-46, **69**
Poblano pepper wraps, 7
Portobello Gorgonzola Beef Tips, 59, **70**
Portobello mushrooms
    and gorgonzola beef tips, 59
    wild mushroom loops, 60–61
Potatoes, red, mashed, 76
Poultry. *See* Chicken; Duck
Preparation times, about, xiii
Prosciutto Vinaigrette, 22

Q

Quail, grilled, 52
Quesadillas, chicken, marinated, 10
Queso blanco
    chicken quesadillas, 10

R

Raspberry
    and chocolate ganache filling, 84
    salsa, 91
    syrup, 85
    vinaigrette, 23
Raspberry Vinaigrette, 23
Recipes. *See also* specific names of recipes
    beer pairings for, about, xiii–xiv
    difficulty ratings for, xiii
    ingredients for, hard to find, 93–95
    preparation times for, xiii
    salting and peppering to taste, xiv
    special equipment needed for, xiii
    wine pairings for, about, xiii
Red Burgundy Gastrique, 61
Red Leaf Lettuce and Asparagus Bundles, 13, **67**
Regina's Black Beans, 79
Rhubarb Compote, 17
Rice
    green, 77
    saffron, 77
    sticky, 77
Rosemary
    crusted salmon, 42
Roulade, dried fruit cambozola, 16

S

Saffron Rice, 77
Salad dressings
    chipotle aioli, 38
    for "Institutional" salad, 14
    vinaigrettes
        balsamic, 24
        currant port, 23
        prosciutto, 22
        raspberry, 23
        tahini, 24
Salads
    cabbage, warm, 20, **66**
    corn, 78

    mixed greens with roulade, compote and vinaigrette, 16–17, **66**
    mozzarella tomato, 18, **70**
    red leaf lettuce and asparagus, 13, **67**
    romaine with dressing ("Institutional"), 14
    spinach
        salmon and strawberry, 19
        sun dried tomato pesto, 15
        tahini vinaigrette, 12
Salmon
    crusted, almond rosemary, 42, **68**
    en croûte, with brie, 2
    salad, with strawberries, 19
Salsas
    pico de gallo, 80
    raspberry, 91
Salt
    types of, xiv
    using to taste, in recipes, xiv
Sashimi, ahi, 45–46
Satay, coconut peanut shrimp, 6
Sauces
    about, 36
    aioli, chipotle, 38
    "Bomb", 38
    caramel, 89
    coconut peanut satay, 6
    gastrique, red burgundy, 61
    hollandaise, James Davis's, 39
    "Mojo", 9
    rhubarb compote, 17
    shrimp essence as base for, 32
    table sauce, Thai, 4–5
Sausages, andouille, on Creole, 48
Seafood. *See* Fish; Shellfish; specific names
Sesame paste. *See* Tahini
Shellfish
    conch chowder, Jamaica jerk, 31, **68**
    crab cakes, 49
    crab stuffed portobello mushrooms, 50
    mussels, stuffed, 3, **66**
    shrimp cakes, Thai, 4–5
    shrimp Creole, Jimmy's, 47–48
    shrimp essence (base), 32
    shrimp satay, coconut peanut, 6
Shrimp
    cakes, Thai, 4–5
    Creole, Jimmy's, 47–48
    essence (base), 32
    satay, coconut peanut, 6

Shrimp Essence, 32
Side dishes
    black beans, Regina's, 79
    corn, 78
    mashed potatoes, 76
    pico de gallo, 80
    rice
        green, 77
        saffron, 77
        sticky, 77
    white beans, Tuscan, 51
Smoked Salmon and Black Pepper Strawberries on Spinach, 19
Smoked Salmon Brie en Croûte, 2
Soups. *See also* Stocks
    butternut bisque, 27
    carrot cumin, 30
    chicken lime tortilla, 28–29
    conch chowder, 31, **68**
    onion, Swiss, 26
Spinach salad, with
    salmon and strawberries, 19
    sun dried tomato pesto, 15
    tahini vinaigrette, 12
Spreads
    pesto, sun dried tomato, 37
    pine nut butter, 54, 55
Squash
    butternut bisque, 27
Steak
    au poivre, 58
    beef tips, 59
Steak au Poivre, 58
Sticky Rice, 77
Stocks
    chef's note about, 33
    chicken, 33
    mushroom, 37
    shrimp essence, 32
    veal, 35
    vegetable, 34
Stout, Winter Warlock Oatmeal
    onions, caramelized, 40
Strawberry and salmon salad, 19
Stuffed Beef Tenderloin Fillet, 57
Stuffed Prince Edward Island Mussels, 3, **66**
Stuffings
    crab, 49
    for mussels, 3

wild mushroom, 60–61
Sun Dried Tomato Pesto, 37
Swiss Onion Soup, 26
Syrups
    raspberry, 85
    red burgundy gastrique, 61

T

Tacos, tilapia, 44, **68**
Tahini Vinaigrette, 24
Tahini Vinaigrette Over Spinach, 12
Tapas, **65**
    beef, Cuban, skewered, 9
    brie en croûte, salmon, 2
    goat cheese terrine, 8
    mussels, stuffed, 3, **66**
    pepper wraps, pablano, 7
    quesadillas, marinated chicken, 10
    satay, coconut peanut shrimp, 6
    shrimp cakes, 4–5
Tenderloin fillet, stuffed, 57
Terrines
    goat cheese, Athena's, 8
Thai Duck with Sugar Snap Peas, 51, **71**
Thai-inspired dishes
    duck, 53
    shrimp cakes, 4–5
    table sauce, 4–5
Thai Shrimp Cakes, 4–5
Thai Table Sauce, 4–5
Tilapia tacos, 44, **68**
Tito Puente Tilapia Tacos, 44, **68**
Tomatoes
    cherry, in bocconcini salad, 18, **70**
    confit, 63
    pico de gallo, 80
    sun dried pesto, 37
Toppings
    dessert
        caramel sauce, tuaca, 89
        crème, French, 89
        raspberry salsa, 91
        raspberry syrup, 85
        whipped ginger cream, 91
    onions, caramelized, 40
    persillade, 40
Tortilla soup, with chicken and lime, 28–29
Tuaca Caramel Sauce, 89

V

Veal
demi-glace, 36
glace de viande, 36
stock, 35
Veal Stock, 35
Vegan dishes
salads
red leaf lettuce and asparagus, 13
spinach, with tahini vinaigrette, 12
sauces
"Bomb" sauce, 38
stocks
mushroom, 37
vegetable, 34
toppings
onions, caramelized, 40
persillade, 40
Vegetable Stock, 34
Vegetarian dishes. *See also* Vegan dishes
crostini, herbed, 21
entrées
moussaka, 63–64
pasta, warm Greek, 62
wild mushroom loops, 60–61, **70**
salads
crostini, herbed, 21
mixed greens with roulade, compote and vinaigrette, 16–17
mozzarella tomato, **70**
romaine with dressing ("Institutional"), 14
spinach, with sun dried tomato pesto, 15
sauces
aioli, chipotle, 38
pesto, sun dried tomato, 37
soups
bisque, butternut, 27
carrot cumin, 30
tapas
goat cheese terrine, Athena's, 8
poblano pepper wraps, 7
Vinaigrettes
balsamic, 24
currant port, 23
prosciutto, 22
raspberry, 23
tahini, 24

W

Warlock Onions, 40
Warm Cabbage with Prosciutto Vinaigrette, 20, **66**
Wild Mushroom Loops with Asparagus and Red Burgundy Gastrique, 60–61, **70**
Wine pairings
about, xiii
index to, 99–100
Wraps, cheese stuffed poblano pepper, 7

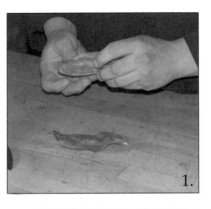
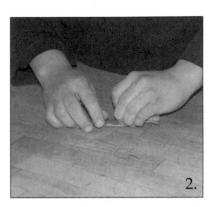

Rolling and cutting fresh basil into thin ribbons called chiffonade.